ELIXXIR

A Brethren Novel – Book Three

DEENA REMIEL

℃ℬ

Decadent Publishing Company
www.decadentpublishing.com

This book is a work of fiction. Names, characters, places, and incidents are the products of the author's imagination or used fictitiously. Any resemblance to actual events, locales or persons, living or dead, is entirely coincidental.

Published by Decadent Publishing Company
Look for us online at:
www.decadentpublishing.com

Printed in the United States of America

~DEDICATION~

To Lindsey and Jowanna, and all women out there who fall for the tortured soul.

~Acknowledgements~

When I set out to write Elixxir, I had no idea the depth that Nathanael and Callie would go until they took me there. Addiction of any kind is a serious matter, and its insidious hold on a person can destroy lives. After meeting Nate in Brethren Beginnings, I knew I couldn't deny his story being told. Callie's hardened adulthood is a testament to her tragic childhood, marred by violence and death. This tough-as-nails woman would need a partner equally as alpha.

The pair makes a dynamic couple, as evidenced by positive remarks from beta readers, friends, and family. I thank them all for their unflagging encouragement and love of my angels regardless how rough around the feathers they may be. I also thank Officer Gomez and a couple of Gilbert police officers standing in line at a Chipotle one evening, for teaching me more about guns. My editors, Rie, Kerry, and Meredith are a winning team that I love and appreciate dearly for teaching me something new with every incarnation of the story.

My husband and children are a constant light in my life, and I couldn't write these stories without their support. Angels really do exist. I live with them.

Prologue

Las Vegas, Nevada
Twenty years ago

They wore masks, carried guns, and they weren't leaving until they got what they came for. That was all Ariana needed to know to scurry silently to the hiding spot her parents had created for her, and her alone, in their bedroom. She considered it rather exciting, at the tender age of six, to have such a special place to play that no one else knew about. Now, at thirteen, it might have very well saved her life.

She'd just gone up to bed, having fed the fish and kissed her parents good night. As the final part of her bedtime routine, she gazed out her window, looking out at the stars in the sky and their reflection on earth, the lights of the Las Vegas Strip a ways off in the distance. That was when an explosion of sound and mayhem erupted from down below. She scrambled to the banister and peered in between the spindles to find two masked men shooting really big guns at everything. And they shouted at her parents to freeze where they were, or they would be dead. One of the men forced her father to his knees, bound and gagged him, then kicked him ruthlessly to the floor. He did the same to her mother, and tied her to the foyer table leg. And all became quiet. Curious to know what these men wanted, she strained to hear over the blood whooshing in her ears as adrenaline coursed through her body.

"Where is it, Joseph? Where's the flask? Tell me now, and I'll let you and your family live. If you don't, I'll start with your pretty wife, here. Shoot her right between the eyes. And if that doesn't motivate you enough, then I'll go looking for your daughter and see what other incentive I can offer you."

Having heard more than enough, she crawled back and hid in her hidey-hole, wondering what was to become of her parents. It seemed a lifetime crept by since she'd first locked herself away, and she needed to know if the masked men got what they were looking for and left. Just as she worked up the courage to open the secret door and investigate, hand on the latch, she heard two loud bangs like a backfiring car. She flinched and catapulted backward, landing deeper into the small space.

At thirteen, there wasn't much Ariana didn't understand. She knew very well at this point that the bangs were not coming from a car, but guns going off right downstairs. She assumed immediately, too, that her parents were most likely dead, murdered by the masked men. What she didn't understand was why. What had they said they wanted? A flask? And would they eventually find her and kill her as well?

Ariana rocked herself while hot tears made a silent pilgrimage down her face. She didn't know how long it finally took for help to find her, since she'd dozed off and on for a while, and had no idea if morning had come yet. At first, she thought the masked men had returned, when harsh banging penetrated her traumatized mind. Instead, official-looking people wearing blue uniforms spoke to her, reached out to her, and waved to her as if to usher her out of the safe haven. But she couldn't move, couldn't respond. With no other choice, they were forced to go in and extract her.

It took days for her to be able to communicate again, during which time she buried her parents, and the family lawyer, Mr. Watkins, explained the inheritance. Among them were retirement funds, real estate holdings, jewelry, and bank accounts, all of which she had no desire to hear anything about. However, one item in particular piqued her curiosity: a flask. The masked men had come to her home looking for it. She never saw it. Rather, Mr. Watkins told her about it, its contents, and how to find its whereabouts should she ever need it. This part of the reading of the will occurred in private after the doctors released her from the hospital and social services placed her into the temporary care of a foster family. Only the lawyer and she met to go over the details.

"I can't begin to tell you how important it is that you keep this a private matter. Your father, with the type of business he ran, sometimes came across nefarious...er...not-so-nice people. He acquired this flask from one of these types of people, and it's probably what led to your parents'...uh, well, anyhow.... You know what it is, what it contains, and how to get it, should you need to do so."

"Mr. Watkins, I'm sorry, but what does it contain again?" she asked, shaking her head to remove the sticky cobwebs from her mind.

"The Elixxir of Life, dear." His kind, soothing voice demonstrated the patience she required since suffering from post-traumatic stress disorder. Loud noises and crowds of people sent her into full-blown panic attacks. Therapy and behavioral conditioning had only just begun, but the doctors promised her it would help. "It is said the flask contains the Elixxir of Life. Anyone who drinks it will supposedly not age any further than they already have, and have amazing strength."

"Where did my dad get this thing, and why do you know so much about it if it's such a secret?"

"It was acquired during one of his trips to the Ukraine. He picked up other items as well, but this item, in particular, had many bidders. Your father offered the highest bid. When he brought it back, it was supposed to go on display in his curiosity shop, but that didn't happen. I guess he believed it too hot an item and it would put the whole shop at risk. So he hid it, well, you know where. As for me, your father has told me many things in confidence over the years. I am...was his attorney, handling all of his personal and business affairs, and now I'm yours, for the time being. So you can confide in me as well. I'm here for you with whatever you need." He paused and smiled, tapping her hand in a very fatherly way.

"Listen, I know the FBI hasn't found your parents' killers yet. They may have a mind to take you out of the home you're in now, and put you in the Witness Protection Program until they do and can bring them to trial. If they offer it to you, I think you should take it and forget everything. The farther away you get from this whole situation and the Elixxir, the better."

"Yes, I guess you're right." She peered absently out the office window and sighed. "Good thing Daddy left his half of the business to Uncle Eddie. At least that's one thing I don't have to worry about."

"Understand you must give up all connections to any family and friends you have right now. But, let's see if that is indeed what the police plan on doing."

"I have no other family. I mean, Uncle Eddie isn't really my uncle. He's just Daddy's partner in the business. But friends? I...I don't know if I can do that." She wrung her hands, remembered to take another breath, and continued. "But if it will keep me alive long enough to see those men brought to justice, then I guess I'm going to have to. You're the boss, Mr. Watkins. But, wait, what about you? Will I not be allowed to know you anymore, either?"

"I'll be available for a time, if you need. Once you've been placed, they'll make sure your name disappears from public records, and you will become someone new."

She frowned and bit her bottom lip. How would she feel not being Ariana Kupi anymore? No more real family picnics, no more real friends who knew all of her deepest secrets and desires. A new name, a new life. Would she be able to carry off a whole new image? Would she feel new on the inside? She had no idea.

But she wanted to live.

The day after their meeting, she discovered that Mr. Watkins had become her champion. The FBI wouldn't offer her the Witness Protection Program while they worked on the case. He, however, took it upon himself to set things up to appear that way for her safety. He protected her assets until such time that the suspects were found, brought to justice, and she could return to her normal life. He found a reputable family to take her in, secured legal documentation from a judge to change her name, and had the records sealed.

She graciously accepted these terms and said goodbye to the life she'd known for thirteen years. She forfeited everything familiar—everything but the knowledge of the Elixxir.

Chapter One

Sedona, Arizona
Present day

"So you're going out with Richie again tonight, huh?" Serena teased. She kicked her feet up on her desk and leaned back in her chair.

"Yes, I'm going out with Richie again. One more date and I'll be on to the next sorry sucker," Callie said nonchalantly, looking into her tiny mirror to fix her lipstick. She heard a *tsk* and looked up. "Oh, now don't start. You know Rule Number One: three dates and out, my friend." She plopped herself down on the chair across from her boss.

A desk piled high with maps and brochures for Serena's Jeep Tour company separated the two, and luckily so, Callie mused, because she wanted to throttle her best friend. The last thing she needed to hear was another lecture on safe sex and her lack of commitment to any lasting relationship. "It's not like I sleep with every guy I date, you know."

"I know, I know. But why? Why are you doing this to yourself? Ever since Kemuel left, you've been acting like this. He's been gone for what, nearly a year now? What on earth happened between you two to make you change into this cold-hearted woman?"

"You're really going to bring him up to me right now? Before my date? You know how I feel about even hearing his name! Thanks. Now you've put me in a mood." She gathered her purse and stood, annoyed. "We're done here. This lovely discussion is over. I've clocked out, so I think I'll go wait for Richie out front. Don't say another word. Just...good night."

Callie didn't wait for a response as she stomped out of the office in her fuck-me pumps, shutting the door with all the restraint she could muster. She strode to the front of the shop and outside to stand under the *Sikes and Sounds of Sedona Jeep Tours* sign. Fussing with her watch, she noted Richie hadn't arrived yet. She worried the pleats of her skirt. Yeah, this one was a little on the trampy side. So what? It went with her trampy shoes. And she had the curvaceous body to flaunt it, so.... She flicked her long, pin-straight hair behind one spaghetti-strapped shoulder, then the other, as she tapped her foot impatiently. Her latest color came from a box of Sexy Hair. Flaming Red, to be exact. But tonight she didn't quite measure up to the sexiness the brand promised on the box. And her trampy clothes weren't cutting it, either. Since she'd dressed, her disposition had soured, and now she regretted the suggestive outfit. That last conversation shifted her all out of sorts, too, and she actually contemplated going home to change.

Where is the bastard, damn it?

Richie screamed into the parking lot in a red Mustang convertible, right as she decided to call her date a bust. He parked in one of the handicapped spots by the front of the shop.

"Hey lady, looks like someone could use a ride."

He flashed his pearly whites as he dragged his hand through his overgrown, curly brown locks. Those curls made him irresistible to women. It was fact. Just the other day, in the grocery store where he worked, she'd overheard three women tell each other so.

"It's about time you showed up, mister." She sauntered over to the curb. "I was about ready to head on home. What's the deal with keeping a lady waiting?"

"Sorry, closing my register gave me grief, so until I figured out the problem, I had to stay. But it's all good. Got us a reservation at Oak Creek Tavern and Grill. Hop in before we're late." Richie shot her a *GQ* smile, leaned over to open her door, and checked his bad self out in the rearview mirror on the way back.

"Sounds great, Richie, thanks."

"You can thank me later, hot lips." He pulled away from the curb.

She said nothing, but raised an eyebrow. *Maybe two dates is enough with this one.*

☙

Dinner turned out to be better than Callie predicted. Richie and she found a lot to talk about, and two hours flew by in the blink of an eye. He drove them back to the store since her car was still there.

"Why don't I follow you back to your place? We've had such a good time, I think. We could continue over some wine."

"I'll follow you back to yours. My place is a mess right now. Redecorating." Rule Number Two: never bring a guy back to the apartment. He'll want to stay over, which leads to Rule Number Three: never let a man sleep over. Go to his place so you can leave when you want.

Richie didn't have a problem with her offer, so within ten minutes they were at his apartment, over a convenience store. The décor surprised her. She expected early bachelor pad, but instead was greeted with a very clean, minimalist, modern design.

"I'm impressed, Richie. Your place isn't at all what I expected. Mind if I take off my shoes? These heels are killing me!"

"Sure, leave them by the front door. Yeah, I like clean lines and no clutter. Here, try this. I think you'll like it. It complements your hair. The color, I mean." He winked at her,

15

putting a glass of merlot in her hand.

She thanked him, and he casually lumbered over to his stereo to put on some mood music. He dimmed the lights and settled in on the couch. She eased herself down next to him.

"So, have you personally given any Jeep tours?"

"Yeah, I've given a couple, but only when we're overbooked, which doesn't happen often since I'm the one in charge of scheduling. What about you? Are you interested in management at the supermarket?"

"Yeah, I'm going for my MBA while I work there." He paused and took her glass. "You know, I think we've done enough talking for now. I know enough about you and you know enough about me. I've wanted to do this since the first time I laid eyes on you."

Richie leaned in, grabbed her face with both hands and locked his lips on hers like a slimy, wet suckerfish. His tentacles—for that's the image his arms produced in her mind—wrapped feverishly around her, his hands groped her ass and back around at her breasts, and she knew there would be marks left behind as souvenirs. After the initial shock, she regained her senses and shoved at his chest to disengage from the jerk.

"Whoa, Richie! You're, uh, running a bit too fast for me here." She scooted off the couch. "I think I'll call it a night." She made it halfway to the door before he tackled her from behind. They fell together to the floor and he quickly flipped her over so they were facing each other. She struggled to get out from under him, but he secured her legs within his and held her wrists tightly in his grip.

"What the hell do you mean, leaving me here with a hard-on? I bought you an expensive dinner, two in fact, counting last night. I talked nice to you. I even let you come to my place. What did you think I would say? 'Toodle-loo! See you soon!' You owe me, Callie," he whispered. "You owe me good. So stop fighting and reciprocate a little here." He pressed down and viciously nuzzled her neck, nipping and licking, while she screamed.

"Stop! Richie, stop! Let me go! I'm not ready for this! Get off of me! No!" She shrieked, and then whispered vehemently, "Don't make me hurt you. I can hurt you."

"Ooh, she likes it rough. Okay then, bruiser, let's make it rough."

He moved ever so slightly to adjust himself. That was all she needed to knee him in the balls, break the hold on her arms, and whack him hard on his ears. As he thrashed about in pain on the floor, she scrambled to the front door. Grabbing at her purse and shoes, she ran to the car as if hell were nipping at her heels. Thankfully, she had left the door unlocked and was able to make a speedy exit. It would take her twenty minutes to get home from his house. Twenty excruciating minutes of hellish memories forced their way to the front of her mind, blending with the evening's debacle.

"No, I won't let you in again! I won't!" Callie shouted to her nightmares. But when Richie said she owed him, it tore a hole in her well-woven fabric of protection and let the horrors of her past slither through to taunt and terrorize her.

She drove on and minded the road, but didn't see it at the same time. Hot tears streamed down her cheeks as she also saw her pretend brother's face through the windshield taunting her that she owed him for coming and upsetting his perfect family structure. She heard him say, clear as the day he'd spoken it, she'd better do whatever he wanted and not tell anyone or he'd make her life a living hell. And then she felt the familiar pressure of this sixteen-year-old fake brother on top of her, forcing himself on her and in her, while her thirteen-year-old body cried and died over and over again.

"You fucking son-of-a-bitch asshole!" She banged her hand against the steering wheel. Had she screamed at Richie the shmuck, or Dennis the rapist-pseudo-brother she'd inherited with the supposedly "good" family courtesy of Mr. Watkins? Both, and every God-damned son-of-a-bitch male on this earth!

Making it home by the grace of God, she locked her front door and wedged a chair under the doorknob. She threw her purse on the floor and ran to the bathroom where she proceeded to throw up the contents of her dinner, and then some. After scrubbing herself raw under the scorching curtain of water, she dressed for bed, made a full pot of tea, and snuggled deep down into her couch.

"Something's gotta change, Callie-girl. You're headed down a dangerous path and there's no denying it. You can't keep this up anymore. No more men. That's it. They're nothin' but trouble anyway. They can't be trusted, they're violent, and they leave you without a second thought."

Well, there had been one man who treated her like gold in her life: her father. Her father who'd been brutally murdered twenty years ago over a stupid trinket that supposedly held some stupid liquid. *What is it? Oh yeah, the Elixxir of Life. That damned flask!* God, how she wished he and her mother were still alive. Her life would have turned out so different from what it currently was—a mess.

Suddenly, a dangerous idea came to her. Dare she even acknowledge it? Should she even try it? How would it feel rolling around her mouth, over her tongue, across her lips? It'd been so long since she'd heard her real name aloud.

"Ariana," she whispered, and quickly covered her mouth with her hands.

ᘓ

I am not opening my eyes yet. If I don't open them, then I don't have to face the anniversary of the worst day in my life. Callie turned over in her bed and groaned. "Oh my God! What the hell?" she yelled. Every muscle in her body ached and her neck and wrists were sore. And then she remembered last night. Richie. *If he ever shows his face near the shop....* What? What would she do? She'd pound his ass into the pavement. But for now, she'd settle for posting a flyer on his supermarket bulletin board extolling his virtues as a caveman. She'd work on that later.

She rolled over again. How would she get through today?

She hated September 21. Her parents had been murdered that day, and she couldn't share that information with anyone she considered even an acquaintance. Not a soul could know the real her, or rather, who she had been twenty years ago. Was there any trace of Ariana left inside her? She had no fucking clue. *Damn!* A day off afforded her no distraction.

Begrudgingly, she got out of bed and put on some sweatpants and a T-shirt. In the bathroom, she stared at herself long and hard while brushing her teeth. Puffy eyes spoke volumes in the mirror. Misery had come to claim her company, but she needed to connect with someone much more positive. Serena had gone to work already. Callie officially had no one right now, and that sucked.

When she sat down in front of her computer, she noticed it'd been left on, and simply clicked on Internet Explorer. Twitter and Facebook were off limits, as were any other sites that would allow her to connect with other people. Despite how much time had passed, she thought she could still be in danger. As long as the murderers were still at large, she couldn't risk being identified. *But there's no harm in surfing the 'net.* Her thoughts had been getting her in a heap of trouble lately, so she gave herself a moment to rethink and reflect.

Nope, no reason not to surf. It's been twenty years. I wonder what Uncle Eddie has done with the shop. I wonder if he's got a website for it. Now these were truly dangerous thoughts. *Don't go there. But who would know if I was simply surfing and came across a website that just happened to be Daddy's old curiosity shop? Nobody would know that I had been there.*

As she talked herself into doing a search, a prickly sensation undulated all over her arms. She was scared and anxious, but mostly curious. Would she find anything? She typed "Kupi and Murati Curiosity Shop" in the search box and closed her eyes, afraid she might find no results. As she peeked through fingers that had involuntarily covered her eyes, she found what she'd been looking for. First on the search list was "Murati Curiosity

Shop."

"So Uncle Eddie took off our last name," she murmured, a bit miffed. He could have left Kupi as part of the store name to honor his dead partner. That would have been nice. *Well, do I enter the site or not? What to do? What to do? Oh, all right! I'll do it!*

She clicked on the link and soon looked into the glowing eyes of a glass skull. Written underneath the skull was Murati's Curiosity Shop. When she clicked on the skull, it opened to the rest of the website. She meandered through the pages, finding all sorts of oddities and legitimate artifacts from all over the world. She found the owner bio page and saw how well Uncle Eddie looked. Time had been kind. And then she saw the "Contact Us" button.

"Oh no, you don't!" she said aloud, just to be sure she heard herself. "Don't you dare click on that button. Do you hear me?" Well, most parts heard her, but not the part that held the mouse. Her finger rebelled and clicked. A live-chat window opened on the screen. "Holy Jesus!" Callie closed out of Internet Explorer and shut down the computer. "What have I done? Man, I'm such a pain in my ass today!" She decided it was not a good day for her to be up and about, so she went back to bed and pulled the covers over her head. She'd stay there until tomorrow eventually came.

ଔ

Tahiti

"Sir, we have news."

"Yes, what is it, Jorge?"

"We got a curious hit on your website, sir. We've traced the signal back to its origin. Double-checked, and with a little research, believe it's the woman you've been looking for. Here are the results, sir." Jorge approached the bamboo desk and held out a folded piece of paper.

"Excellent, excellent! Well, hello, long-lost little girl, now a woman. It took you long enough to surface, didn't it? Looks like your hide-and-seek game is all but over because I gotcha now! Ha! Jorge, get the helicopter ready. I've cut my vacation short. I want to leave within thirty minutes."

"Your destination, sir?"

"Sedona Airport, Arizona. And make sure my limo is ready when we arrive."

"Yes sir," Jorge replied and left quickly.

He took his gun out of the desk drawer and loaded it. "Oh, my dear Ariana. You may have cheated death once, but you're not going to be so lucky this time. You're the last thread, the last piece of a family I've long despised. I've imagined for so long a world without any Kupis left in it. And now my dream will finally come true! If only I could have gained custody of you twenty years ago, this could have been over with already. Ah, well, what did I expect after being investigated by the FBI? Not exactly the proper father figure, now was I?" He aimed his gun at an imaginary target. "Pow! Right between the eyes, just like your mother! No wait, that's too fast. Maybe I'll kill you the way I killed your father. Pow! One in the left lung. Pow! One in the right lung. Pow! One right through the heart. Or better still, maybe I'll let you decide how you die."

Chapter Two

*K*emuel and Raphael laughed up a storm as they entered Serena's Sikes and Sounds of Sedona Jeep Tour shop. It was too early for customers, but some of the guides had already begun trickling in. Raphael opened the door to her office with a bit of drama and flair.

"Honey! I'm home!" He topped it off with a big toothy grin. Serena looked up from her desk with a mixture of a smile and a grimace. The smile was for her husband. The grimace was for the cad, Kemuel.

"Hey!" She jettisoned from her chair and leapt into his awaiting arms. "Did you just get back? How was the Healing Conference? I missed you!" She didn't give him a chance to respond as she planted a searing kiss on his lips.

"Ahem! Get a room, you two."

She released Raphael from her clutches and stared at his buddy with eyes she hoped bored holes through his lunkhead heart.

"What? What'd I do? I just came in!"

"You've been gone for a long time, no goodbye, no information about where you were going, nothing. And you have the audacity to walk into my establishment, where Callie works, as though you were only in here yesterday. You are unbelievable, Kemuel."

"Oh, that. Yeah, well, it couldn't be helped. When the boss man says *jump*, you say *how high.?* E.L. needed me back at base, interviewing recruits for the new Warrior to take Seraphiel's place. You know we've been down a Brother for a while now. The Brethren work best in triads—three Protectors, three Saviors, and three Warriors. Plus, I got a new assignment."

"You couldn't call, or let one of the others know, or Callie? For God sakes, Kemuel, where is your sense of responsibility to the woman? Your sense of decency?"

"The Brethren knew, but no one else could. Jeez, Serena, I was only gone a couple of days!"

She glared at her husband. "You knew? You are so in the doghouse, dearest. As for you," she said, turning back to Kemuel. "Are you kidding me? A couple of days? It's been months!"

"Aw, man!" he groaned, hitting his palm against his forehead. "I forgot about the freakin' time differential. Shit, she's gonna have my balls for breakfast."

She shook her head in exasperation. "I wouldn't worry. She's so not interested in your balls in any way, shape, or form. Jesus, Kemuel." She pinched the bridge of her nose, trying to clear the incredulity from her mind. "All right, listen. She doesn't come in until seven. You better get your ass out of here before she sees you. And if I were you, I'd spend the day working on how you're going to get back into her good graces. I gotta warn you, though. She'll probably not even give you the time of day. You don't know what you've done to her. She's different. Changed. Hardened in a way. Whether she wants you to or not, you're responsible for fixing her. Do the right thing and explain things to her. Tell her the truth about who you are. I want my best friend back, Kemuel. Whatever it takes."

"I'll do what I can, Serena. Sorry. I didn't mean to hurt her." He gave her a troubled look, shook Raphael's hand, and left the shop.

"About that doghouse...." Raphael started.

"You're in it until I get home. Then I'm really gonna make you suffer, you very bad angel, you." She sent him a private message through their telepathic, threaded connection. A promise of wanton pleasure after a bit of slow, seductive torture.

CB

Kemuel deemed himself worthy of an ass-kicking. His latest assignment was supposed to be a cakewalk—find the location of the flask containing the Elixxir of Life, take possession of it, and return it back to base for safe-keeping. Well, there'd be no cakewalk now. He'd be lucky to get within a thousand miles of the flask at this point.

Damn his stupidity! He should have told her he'd be away on business, but it slipped his mind, and he didn't think she would care anyway, free spirit that she was. It was only a couple of days! But not to her. Jesus, did he ever screw up. She'd never tell him where to find the flask, let alone want to see him at this point. He would have to present a clear, logical argument for his behavior, give her lots of presents, and pour on the charm. He could do that. He was real good at charm.

CB

The alarm proved to be no friend come Monday morning. It wouldn't stop buzzing. Callie picked it up and threw it clear across the room. Before hitting the far wall, it managed to nail a delicate glass figurine, smashing it into a thousand pieces.

"Well, shit." She got up to get the dustpan and broom, and swept her mess away. She fell back against her bed and ruffled her hair. "All right, sister, you promised yourself you'd change, so here we are at Day One. Get your act together, put some decent clothes on, and paint a smile on your face. Today is the first day of the rest of your life!" She sat up and smiled a cheesy, fake smile at her reflection in the dresser mirror and got ready for work.

She saw things in a whole different light by the time she downed her coffee and ate her English muffin. After tossing her plate and mug in the sink, she did a final check of her face and hair in the foyer mirror, opened the door, and slammed straight into a wall of man.

"Whoa," said a rich, baritone voice.

"Oh, my God! I'm so sorry! I didn't know you were...." Her next words were frozen on her tongue as she identified the mammoth creature in front of her.

Kemuel.

Too stunned to move, she looked straight into his jade-colored eyes, momentarily lost in the memory of how they once made her knees turn to jelly. The memory faded quickly, and she smirked as her knees held her steady and strong. Having regained her composure, she saw a huge bouquet of flowers in his hands. Crushed flowers, now.

"Hello, Callie. I—"

Before he could say another word, she backed up and slammed the door in his face.

Leaning against it, she closed her eyes, wishing that she'd simply imagined him, and it was really the guy from the florist down the street. She turned and looked through the peephole. No such luck. Kemuel stood there, all right. *What the hell is he doing here? Maybe if I stay in here long enough, he'll give up and go away. No, be realistic, woman. You're gonna have to throw him out. Just do it.*

Slowly, she opened the portal to Hell to find him still standing there in all of his six-foot-four, god-like glory, looking shell-shocked. She hadn't forgotten how perfection had shined down upon him, kissing his head with pure white strands of hair, and blessed him with a muscular build meant to be scaled by her. She also hadn't forgotten being left high and dry for months on end, either.

"Callie, I...."

"Shut up," she said softly, venomously. "I will say this once and once only, so you'd better listen good. You have some fucking nerve showing up here after all this time with a bouquet of stinkin' flowers. If I see you anywhere near my place or the shop, I'm gonna call the fucking police and have you fucking arrested for...for...being an asshole! Now, get the hell out of my way. I've gotta go to work." She pushed past him, slammed her front door, and wished her eyes flashed real death rays.

"But...sweetheart, please, you gotta let me explain!" he called to her, and quickly followed to her car. She noticed and began running. With her door thankfully still unlocked from last night, she threw herself into her seat, locked it immediately, switched on the ignition, and tore out of the parking lot. When she looked in her rearview mirror, a plume of dust gave way to a vision of Kemuel caked in red dirt.

愉

"You will not believe who I just left standing in my parking lot!" Callie slammed Serena's office door closed and pulled the privacy shade down. She turned to face her and continued, saying incredulously, "Kemuel!"

"Really?"

"Uh huh, asshole! When the *hell* did *he* get back? What does he think? We can just pick up where we left off?" She sat down on a chair, her right knee bobbing up and down frantically.

"Hmm."

"I mean, he's been gone forever! And he thinks he can waltz right back into my life with some stinkin' flowers and that will make everything okay? What an idiot, right?" She got up and paced the office.

"Oh yeah, complete idiot. I'm right there with you, Cal."

"So, you know what I tell him?" She sat down again.

"No, sweetie. What?"

"I basically tell him to fuck off and leave me the hell alone. And the best part of it all, when I saw him, my knees didn't go weak. I'm so over him, it's not even funny. Now it's up to him to take the hint."

"I'm so happy for you! Here," Serena said, as she whisked out a couple of water bottles from her tiny fridge. "Let's drink to your new beginnings!"

Callie smiled broadly as they "clinked". New beginnings, she mused. *Yeah, I know how to do that.*

ဆ

"What am I going to do, Raph?" Kemuel asked, and hunkered down on the sofa in Raphael's living room, munching on a bag of chips. "She's never gonna let me near her to even ask about the damn flask. I gotta find that Elixxir, and she's the only one who knows where it is."

"Damn shame you blew her off like you did."

"Hey, what am I here for, anyway? To shack up with some chick and play family? That's not what I signed up for. That wasn't in the contract. I'm here to wage war against evil. I'm a Warrior. That's what I do. I'm thinking I should pass this assignment off to another Warrior. What do you think?"

"Sounds like a plan. I would also ask you to apologize to Callie. Think of what I have to live with, my brother. She and Serena are like sisters. And it's been a hellish amount of months I've had listening to them bitch and moan over you. I now know the myriad ways you can be turned into dead meat. I need you out of my life, man! Figuratively, of course."

"Of course. All right, all right." Kemuel got up and tossed the empty chip bag in the garbage can. "I'll go make nice. But that's all. I'm done with attachments, and I'm giving the assignment to Nathanael. This is right up his alley, anyway. He's the bounty hunter. He's got a knack for sniffing people and things out."

"You're right. Good call." Raphael smacked his hands together and grinned. "I can't wait to *not* talk about you at dinner anymore!"

Kemuel punched him soundly on the shoulder, and as he headed out the door, winked and flipped him the finger.

Chapter Three

*W*hen Kemuel entered his apartment, it confirmed the fact he'd been gone a long time. An immediate musty odor greeted him when he opened the door, and he could see a thick layer of dust coating every exposed surface. *Great*, he thought, as he fought with a spider web. *I'd better call someone to clean this place up.*

He didn't dare open the refrigerator. The cleaning service could have that bit of fun. Proceeding to his bedroom and his wardrobe, he reached in and grabbed a couple days' worth of clothing, stuffed it in his saddlebag, and adjusted the sword resting against his back. It would be best to stay at a hotel during the detox. He called a company and scheduled them to come the following day. Riding his Harley Cross Bones, he headed to the cheap hotel up the road.

He didn't know exactly how to apologize. Flowers had been a major fail, but maybe jewelry or a Coach handbag would work? Or maybe a Rolex watch. Or maybe all of the above. Hell, he'd think about that later. Right now he had to get Nathanael on board with his plan.

ଓ

It wound up being a nightmarish kind of day at work, which

worked out quite well, since it kept Callie's mind off the shambles of her personal life. Richie hadn't been seen anywhere near the shop. After telling Serena about their date and the attempted rape, her best bud called a sheriff friend of hers. He assured her he would put the fear of God in the man, but should anything further happen to escalate the situation, he would haul his ass straight to jail. Kemuel hadn't shown up at the shop, either. Good thing, too. He was the last person she wanted to see right now.

Closing time presented a problem. She would have the rest of the night to obsess over Kemuel's sudden reappearance. "Heading out, Serena," she said, peeking into the office. "Have a good night, and thanks for everything. I appreciate it."

"If there's anything more I can do, you know I'm right here for you, girlfriend." Callie smiled, gave her a wink, and headed for home.

ଔ

With the door good and locked behind her, Callie kicked off her shoes and sorted the mail. Spaghetti and meat sauce leftovers would be dinner. Out of the corner of her eye she saw a flashing light. *A message? At home? How strange.* Anyone that knew her always called on her cell phone. Puzzled, she approached the machine sitting on the corner of the kitchen counter and pressed Play. The voice startled her. The man groaned and grunted, and each pained word grew fainter. The meaning, however, transmitted loud and clear.

"Ariana Kupi, this is Mr. Watkins, your lawyer. I've been trying to get you on your cell phone, but it keeps saying your inbox is full. Your identity has been compromised. Whatever you do, do not use your computer or access the Internet. Pack a bag and leave your home as soon as you hear this. Run, Ariana, and don't look back. I didn't tell them, Ariana. I didn't tell them anything."

"Oh, my freakin' God! Mr. Watkins," she murmured, holding

on to the kitchen counter for purchase. "What do I do? What do I do?" Her mind went from zero to sixty in two seconds flat. She flung a backpack from atop her bedroom closet onto her bed and opened it. Drawers were hastily opened and clothes thrown in a haphazard manner. *Where to go? The police?* She'd lost faith in them over the twenty years they couldn't find her parents' killers. *Serena's? Yeah, that would be good. Raphael is in the security business. He can get me hidden.*

Zipping up the bag, she slung it over her shoulder. Someone knocked at the front door. She froze, and heard another knock, and another. Very insistent, but very friendly-like, as if to throw her off. She wanted to run, but she couldn't move. Fear had turned her into a stone statue.

"Callie, please open up, would ya?"

Recognizing Nathanael's voice, she sighed in relief. *Thank God! Kemuel's friend could be very useful.* He worked for Brethren Security along with Kemuel and Raphael. Dare she ask for help and get him involved in her mess? She didn't have a choice right now. She had to get out of this apartment and find lost. Then, she could lose him.

She opened up the door as far as the chain lock would allow. Verifying that friend, not foe, stood on the other side, she closed the door, unlocked it, and reopened it. She grabbed him by the collar with one hand, and with a confused look, he allowed her to push him back toward his motorcycle.

"Don't say anything or do anything except strap down my backpack and take me to a hotel, now! It's a matter of life and death, so hurry the fuck up!"

"What the...? No problem."

Nathanael's alert system went full-tilt. He deftly secured her sack and hopped on the bike in under fifteen seconds. He didn't know what was going on, but if Callie said life or death, if Kemuel's free-spirited ex-girlfriend was asking *him* for help, it had to be serious.

He ripped up the road to a nearby hotel, and after checking

in two adjoining rooms under an assumed name, the frantic woman tore a key from his hand and ran up the steps to the second-floor room. By the time he came in, he found her crouched on the floor in between the bed and the wall, trembling, and pissed as hell.

Dropping his own pack on the floor, he hurried over to her and kneeled down before her.

"Stupid, stupid, stupid, stupid, stupid...."

"Jesus Christ, Callie, what the hell's going on? Tell me, so I can help you."

She met him with silence.

"Come on. Whatever it is, you can tell me. I won't judge, I won't betray your confidence. I can keep you safe. But I gotta know what we're dealing with here, so I can plan our next move. Okay?"

More silence. He got up and left her. One thing Kemuel had said about her when he briefed him on the assignment, she was as stubborn as a mule. She would tell him when she was good and ready. He bristled at the fact he'd need to wait. He hated waiting, he hated secrets, and he hated not being in control.

In the meantime, he stepped out into the hallway to try to make sense of everything that had occurred over the last twenty minutes. He thought about Callie, the enigma. He didn't really know much about her. They had met at Raphael and Serena's wedding. They'd sat at the same table, right next to each other, in fact, but whenever he asked her certain questions, like about her past or growing up, she always evaded them. Kind of like the way he had evaded talking about his. So alike, they were. The only difference between the two, as far as he could figure, was his secret, being a Brethren Warrior angel and immortal, had to be bigger than hers. He had respected her privacy. A lot of people on earth had shitty upbringings and preferred to keep it quiet and hidden. But if today's situation had anything to do with her past, she would have to spill it.

Callie berated herself. How did this happen? What could I have done? Holy shit. I'm such a fucking idiot! The Contact Us button on Uncle's website. Damn it! I alerted someone, somewhere. Now, here she sat with Nathanael, in a hotel room of all places, having to come up with some freakin' lie to cover her ass. She couldn't tell him the truth about her past, or the existence of something as monumental and preposterous as the Elixxir of Life. He'd think her totally nuts. They didn't know each other well enough for him to go on faith, so she'd have to come up with something believable or plain old nothing at all. And then she'd have him take her to Raphael. She trusted him. He would surely have a place in mind, far from here, to hide out in while someone staked out her apartment and found out who wanted her dead.

"Nathanael," she called, standing finally. "Nathanael!"

He rushed back inside and crossed the room to stand before her. His stormy green eyes bore holes straight to her heart and it ached. Emotion like that took her completely off guard.

"Are you ready to tell me what's going on?"

She took an unsteady, deep breath. "No. I need you to take me to Raphael's. He'll know where there's a good place to hide."

"Hide? Listen, if your life is in danger, you need me. I'm a bounty hunter by trade. A military man, through and through. This is what I'm trained for, not Raphael. I'm the best equipped to take care of you, and I'd like to. Let me do this for you. Let me protect you and fight off the bad guys."

"I...I don't even know who the bad guys are!" She raised her hands to the ceiling in frustration and then slapped them against her thighs. "I just know they're after me. And as for you, the only reason I'm here with you right now is due to a case of poor timing on your part. I was running out, while you were, well, I don't really know what you were doing at my door. Maybe you're the one who should be explaining yourself to me." She assumed a defiant stance with hands on her hips and waited.

"Kemuel sent me over. To, you know, apologize for skipping out without telling you first."

"Uh, huh." Figured. The jackass had sent someone else to do

his dirty work. "Apology not accepted because it doesn't matter anymore. He left. I'm done with him. I'm done with the lot of you. So you can take that message back to him and shove it up his ass. All I need from you right now is a ride to Raphael's, and then I'll thank you to be on your way." She grabbed her backpack and headed toward the door.

"You may not know *who* these guys are that are after you, but I know you know *why* they're after you."

She stopped and turned around with a glare. "You're not gonna let this go, are you?"

"Nope. Not when it comes to a threat on your life, I'm not."

"You have your secrets, I have mine," she said. "Suffice it to say that I need to be hidden for a while until they give up their search. I figured that with Serena and Raphael living in the safe house at the moment, they could find another hidey-hole for me to stay in until this blows over."

"You think that's all it's going to take? You're so naïve," he said. "Can you tell me this much? Are you into anything illegal?"

"Oh, heavens, no! There are things from my past that I can't discuss...with you or anyone. So please stop pushing."

He pinched the bridge of his nose as he closed his eyes. She didn't care that she frustrated him. She wasn't ready for him to know the truth. She might never be.

"Hey? Did you see where I threw my phone?" She started looking under the bed and nightstand. "I need to call Serena."

"Don't bother. They're hosting a group of out-of-towners in their home for a big conference that includes multiple tours of Sedona."

"Damn it! I forgot. Well, good for them, bad for me." She sat back down on the bed, totally exasperated. *Face it, you need Nathanael.* As much as she didn't want to, she needed him. *He's right. He's the only one who can do what I need done: protect me, and get the bastards who want me dead.*

"Callie...."

"Okay! Okay! I see I'm left with no other choice but you, so all right. It'll have to do."

"How very generous of you," he snickered.

"What do you want from me?" She raised her arms in frustration. "I've spent months despising every molecule of Kemuel's being. You can't possibly expect me to fall at your feet in abject gratitude, you being a close friend of his. You want a softer, more gentle Callie, you're gonna have to look elsewhere. She abandoned me when he did." She charged into the bathroom and shut the door, leaving Nathanael to chew on that tidbit for a while.

Chapter Four

*D*amn it all! He wants something I can't give. Full disclosure. What am I going to say? How much of my life should I reveal? As little as possible to get the job done. Callie looked at herself in the mirror. She splashed cool water on her face and toweled it dry. Her bloodshot, violet eyes asked much of her. Got your story straight? She nodded, pinched her cheeks for color, and opened the bathroom door resolutely.

"I've decided to share some information with you." Nathanael raised a brow as she closed the bathroom door behind her and sat on the edge of the king-sized bed. "Now don't get all excited. I'm prepared to tell you only what is absolutely necessary for you to know. My life depends on secrecy. I'm sorry."

"Seriously, your life depends on me knowing everything about you, but I won't push it, yet. Tell me what I need to know now, and we'll figure out the rest as we go along. It's not the way I operate, but I'm not about to release you to face God-knows-what. Tell you what I'll do." He pulled a chair over right in front of her, and sat down knee to knee. "Just to make things square, I'll share one of my secrets, and after, you can tell me something about what's going on. Sound like a deal?"

"Why are you being so nice to me? I treat you like shit, and you're being nice."

"I'm a professional. It's part of my professional duties."

She scoffed. "As long as you know I don't like you, okay?"

"Got it. I don't like you either, if that makes you any happier. So should I spill my beans or no?"

"By all means, spill away." She clasped her hands on her lap and looked him square in the eyes. *My, but they're the greenest eyes I've ever seen. Like—like emeralds. Oh, shut up, Callie! You don't like him.*

"Well, I'm a military man, as I said earlier. I've been on many black-ops' missions. Well, one of those times, we failed. I failed. I miscalculated the timing of the extraction." He paused and frowned. "I lost my entire team."

"Whoa. How many of you were there?"

"Five, plus me. Five guys whose families would never see them again."

"How awful. I'm so sorry. But thank goodness you survived."

"Yeah, well, I certainly don't feel very thankful to have to live each day knowing they will never walk this earth again because of me."

"Sounds like you've got a case of survivor's guilt."

"I said I'd tell you a secret. I didn't say you could analyze me." He got up from his chair and went to his saddlebag. He reached in and took out a water bottle. "You want one?"

"Well, you don't have to bite my head off. I'll keep things nice and shallow for you, all right? And yes, I'd love one."

"I'm sorry. Didn't mean to be so touchy. Your turn on the hot seat. Spill it, Red."

"Well, you were right. I don't know who, but I know why those guys want me. I suspect they want something that belonged to my father and now belongs to me. I've been able to hide from them for a long time, but apparently they've found me and want what's mine. I'm afraid they'll want me dead, too, once they get it."

"Are you gonna tell me what it is?"

"Nope."

He sighed and raked his hands through his hair.

"Okay then, where is it?"

She pursed her lips and shook her head.

"Jesus, Callie! How can I help if I don't know what they're after?" He jumped up and paced the floor.

"You don't need to know what they're after. All you need to know is that they want it and it's mine, and they can't have it. Ever." She jumped up. "Oh, shit. I left the envelope. Damn it all! Nathanael, I left an envelope with vital information inside it back in a lockbox at my apartment. You gotta take me back there so I can get it. I won't let them have it!" She stalked over to the door, picking up her purse along the way.

"Whoa, whoa! Where do you think you're going?" He grabbed her arm. She turned toward him.

"I'm going back to the apartment really fast, and you're taking me there. I need that envelope. If it gets in their hands, I'm done for."

"You're one crazy chick, you know that? First you shanghai me into bringing you here, and now you want to go back? They know where you live. You're insane!"

"You don't get it." She pulled him out the door, down the stairs, and out to his motorcycle. "All the information about the...what they want, is in it. Mr. Watkins, my lawyer, told me so. Now hurry up."

She heard him mumbling something unintelligible as he strapped on his helmet and gave her his spare. "Listen closely. When we get there, you are to do exactly what I tell ya, you hear?"

"Got it, now turn this thing on and let's go!" How could she have been so stupid as to leave that information behind? *It's my lifeline, a key to the past, and the only evidence I have that the flask exists.*

"Hold on," he shouted, and revved the engine.

She tried grabbing hold of his T-shirt, but there wasn't enough give to the material. She wrapped her arms around his waist instead, and shook her head. *Those damn muscles! Can't he find an appropriate-sized shirt, for God's sake?* She tapped him on the shoulder to let him know he could shove off.

Ψ

Nathanael rode up to the entrance of the apartment complex and cut the engine. He parked in a shady area about forty or so spots down and across from her garden apartment. Taking off his helmet, he turned to find Callie removing hers and shaking out her flaming red hair. *Boy, is she a stunner. It's a shame I want to throttle her most of the time.* He dismounted the bike.

"Remember. Do as I say. Nothing more, nothing less."

"Got it, Captain." She got off the bike, as well, and saluted him.

"Don't call me that. Ever. I left the military a lifetime ago." He looked her dead in the eyes and stared her down. "I'm a bounty hunter now. That's all."

She didn't cower or back down, but met his piercing gaze with equal intensity. "Yes, sir," she hissed. "My mistake, sir." She challenged him in a test of wills and wouldn't budge. Well, neither would he. He inched closer until he stood a hair's breadth away from her face.

"Are we really gonna stand here and have a contest to see who's got the bigger balls? Because you've already lost. Save your bratty aggression for when you really need it. All right?" He backed off, put his hands on her shoulders, and turned her toward her apartment. "Now stay close and follow me."

She said nothing, just sneered. He grabbed her hand as they crossed the parking lot, and it spoke volumes. Cold, clammy, and trembling. She really knew how to put up a good front. He chose to ignore the fear she hid. It wouldn't do either of them any good to expose it right now.

Callie stepped onto the curb, and a massive explosion of sudden heat and fire thrust shards of glass, wood, and other debris into the air to rain down upon the two of them and any other innocent bystanders. The force of the blast threw them both to the ground a good ten feet from where they'd just been. Nathanael shook it off, while other people scurried about aimlessly, screaming, not knowing exactly what to do. He quickly sat up and scrambled over to Callie, a few feet away. She lay on her back, not moving, eyes closed. Pieces of building, like concrete confetti, lay all about her.

"Callie! Can you hear me?" He pressed two fingers to the side of her neck and checked her vitals. She had a strong pulse. He did a quick examination of her body. Tiny nicks and abrasions dotted her arms, legs, and face, but her head wasn't bleeding, nor were there any big bumps. The cuts sprinkled his arms and face as well, but they would disappear shortly. "Damn it, wake up!" He brushed away tiny bits of building from her face to reveal a paleness starkly contrasted to her violent, red hair. Her plump, rose-stained lips had parted slightly as little puffs of breath escaped. Even with the mess all around them and the scrapes she received from the blast, he thought she still looked beautiful, like an exotic fairy.

She stirred and groaned, rubbing her head. "Oh.... Jesus." He helped her up to a sitting position. "What happened?"

"There was an explosion. From there." He pointed at the fiery, gaping hole that used to be her garden apartment. "Either this was a total coincidence, or the bad guys got what they were looking for and sent you a pretty strong message."

"Oh, my God. My apartment," she murmured, her eyes wide as she looked upon the devastation. All sorts of people from the complex crowded around to look at the blaze and help those who needed it. Some approached him to see if the two of them were okay. He assured them they were. One of them called the police and fire department. Callie's face turned ashen. She grabbed hold of his arms as though she were clinging to the edge of a cliff.

"We need to get out of here. They could still be around, watching, but are you all right to stand up and walk on your own?"

"I think so, and if not, too damn bad. I don't want to be here right now anyway, with everyone staring at us. So get us out of here." She looked at him with pleading eyes that could move mountains, and probably had.

He held out a hand for her to grab and pulled her up gently. Some good Samaritans were headed their way. He deftly waved them off. "It's okay. Help the others. We're fine. We're just gonna go and clean ourselves up. No real harm done. Thank you. Boy, I feel bad for whoever rented that apartment." He nodded to various onlookers as they hurried away, down the parking lot to his bike. He scanned the area for anything suspicious, but there were no cars sitting idly with people inside, nor could he see anyone on the rooftops. Whoever had done this probably timed it to go off after they left.

He had to give the woman props. Obviously shaken beyond words, she still held it together, just enough not to raise any flags with the nosy neighbors. Fire engines and police vehicles screamed past as they reached his bike. No one would be the wiser about the two of them.

He sat on his motorcycle and waited for her to climb on. And waited some more. He turned to find her standing there, staring blankly at the bike.

"Let's go." She looked at him, nodded, and climbed on the back. Again, he waited. "Grab on to me, now." Her arms didn't embrace him. He reached back and grabbed them himself. They dropped. *What's going on with her?* "Callie, what gives?"

"I...I can't do it." She shook her head, looking puzzled.

"Shit." He got up from his seat. "All right, listen to me. Scoot forward and turn around so you're facing the back of the bike." She did as he told her. "Now I'm gonna sit back down, and I want you to straddle my lap. Then, rest yourself against my chest. Okay?"

He helped her maneuver herself onto him. *God help me, but her body fits like a freakin' glove! Breathe, man. You don't need a distraction like this right now. Just get her back to the hotel and figure out the next steps.* Her legs crossed around his hips, and she rested snugly against him. Her arms hung limply at his sides. He started the bike as more fire engines and police cars rushed by.

There was much to ponder on the ride back. What exactly was in that envelope? Did the people after her find it and take it before the blast, or had it been destroyed? Or, did it survive the blast, without being found? He hated being a pessimist, but more than likely, they'd gotten what they wanted. He'd have to go back later tonight and do a little recon on his own.

After a continuous checking of his side mirrors and taking many unexpected turns to shake off anyone who might be following, he finally pulled into their hotel's parking lot, found a shady spot to park the bike, and turned off the Fatboy's rumbling engine. Curiously, the vibrations of the beastly machine continued. He checked, and the engine was definitely off. And then he realized where the shaking originated from. Callie. Wracked with sobs, her whole body shook up and down.

"Hey, girl. It's gonna be fine." He instinctively rubbed her back. "I told you I'd help you. Right? And look, we survived a pretty big blast back there. That's a good sign that things are gonna work out."

She looked up at him with tears streaming down, untamed. Dripping mascara dramatized an already intense situation. She shook her head. Between sobs, she managed to speak her mind.

"It's not...gonna work out. They got...the envelope. I know they did. Why else...torch the place?" She swiped at her tears. "No, they got it, and I'm next. They'll come for me next." She tried to ease herself off of his lap, but he stopped her.

He reached up and held her cheeks in his palms. "Now you listen to me. You are too much of a pain in the ass to give up before this show has played itself out." One corner of her mouth lifted for a slight smirk. "And I can promise you, no one will get to you on my watch. No one. I know you're scared right now. But can you put a little faith and trust in me to see this operation to a successful conclusion?"

She shrugged. He sighed and dropped his hands. "Let's go to

the room and finish this discussion, because, my dear, there is a lot more that we need to discuss."

"Okay." She wiped away the lingering tears and when she moved to get up, he let her.

They climbed the stairs in silence, one step at a time, but he noticed Callie wincing each time she lifted a foot to the next tread. Without fanfare, he picked her up and cradled her in his arms while taking the rest of the stairs two at a time, and didn't set her down until they were inside the bedroom area of the suite. He immediately went to the bathroom and ran the hot water. Leaning against the door jamb, he pointed to the shower stall.

"Get in. It will do you a world of good. When you're done, we'll talk."

"Thank you." She looked down at her feet and wrung her hands.

"Don't thank me yet." He snickered. She looked up. "When I say talk, I mean, you're gonna tell me everything you know. Full disclosure. It's that or I hit the road, and you're on your own."

She frowned. "What happened to 'I told you I'd help you'? Seeing it through to a successful conclusion?"

"I will see it through to a successful conclusion, on my terms. I won't help any more, Red, without knowing exactly what we're up against. Take as long as you need in there. I'm not going anywhere yet."

He closed the French doors separating the living room from the bedroom, strode to the door, opened it, and leaned against the railing. It was hot as hell outside, but even hotter inside. Having felt nearly every curve of her body through their clothing on the way over, he couldn't help but imagine how they'd react under his hands, in the shower. *Shit.*

He took out his cell phone, pushed number two on the speed dial and waited. "Hey, Joe! How you doin'? Can you meet me at the Sedona Suites on Main Street? I need to bend your ear on something. Five minutes. Great. And get ready to do some sparring. I got some wicked energy to work off."

"Hey, man, how you been?" Joe extended his hand and Nathanael shook it heartily.

"Been better, but what else is new? How about you? How's life been treating ya? I know you're rehabilitating demons these days. Are they behaving?"

"Not really. They all wanna stay evil for some reason." He shrugged and laughed.

"I told you you'd have a tough go of it. Not every demon has a conscience like you."

"That's right. I'm special."

"You're special, all right. Hey, thanks for coming. I wanted to run something by you. See what you thought."

"Shoot. You know I'm good for a little intrigue. So where are we working out?"

"In here. Come on." He opened the door to his hotel room. "Some shit's going down with a woman I'm helping. It has to do with a mission I'm on. I need you to keep an eye out for any demonic energy above and beyond the ordinary around here. They seem to like you for some reason." He laughed and threw a left jab, hitting his old friend squarely on the jaw.

"It must be my pretty face." Joe answered with a right hook that connected with Nathanael's cheek. "What's going on?"

The two began sparring in earnest.

"She knows where it is, Joe." Jab. "The Elixxir. And someone wants it bad enough to blow up her apartment. I gotta convince her to tell me where the damned thing is and get it back to the Beyond or there could be big time trouble."

"No kidding? *The* Elixxir? How the hell did she acquire *that* flask of temptation?"

"She inherited it from her father. He's dead and the people after it want her dead, too. The whole situation reeks of Evil."

"I'll keep an eye out for ya', sure. Now, give me your best shot."

"Remember, you asked for it."

ℭ𝔰

Hot water sluiced over the scraped and bruised curves of Callie's shoulders, elbows, hips, and knees. It stung for a minute, and brought to her attention how very lucky she was to be alive. Closing her eyes, she lost herself in the soothing pounding against her back. She slid down the shower wall, her legs unable to hold her up any longer, and let the water continue to barrage her body with its therapeutic fingers.

Shit. I almost died back there. What a freakin' mess. And now I gotta tell him everything or he'll split. I can tell him about my parents, the murders, about changing my entire life to someone new. I can tell him they were murdered for...what? What do I tell him? He mustn't know the truth. He'd either think me totally insane, or believe the story and want to steal the flask at the first opportunity. The damn thing is probably filled with plain old tap water, for Christ's sake! No, Mom and Dad wouldn't have been killed over tap water. That monster who's out to get me knows there's something to the lore.

Shaking her head in disgust, she turned off the shower, inched her way up to standing, and toweled off. She opened the door to the bedroom and cursed, remembering her backpack was still on the sofa. The sun had begun to set on what had been a most disastrous day. *At least Nathanael has finally given me some privacy.* She proceeded through the doors to the living room of the suite to retrieve her clothes.

But no sooner had she thought herself alone than the door opened and the beast appeared. And he had someone with him. A tall, sinewy man. Both were dripping from head to toe in sweat. She tugged her towel tighter, a bit self-conscious of her battered body, and the simple fact that she didn't go parading around in a towel every day for all eyes to see.

"Uh, excuse me, but I'm changing here."

"Oh, I'm so sorry, miss! I'll be seeing ya, Nate. I'll look into that matter we spoke of and get back to you." The mystery man shook his hand and left.

"Who the hell was that, *Nate*, and what on earth were you doing while I showered? It looks like you took one yourself, but in your own sweat!"

He swiped his forehead with his forearm. "That's Joe, an old friend. I needed to ask him something and we got to sparring."

"Let me get this straight. We just lived through an explosion that could have killed us both, and you decide to trade punches with an old friend? You're insane, you know that? Certifiable. A bounty hunter who's addicted to physical pain and thinks he's invincible." She stalked over to him and began looking his body over.

"Like what you see, Red?" He raised his eyebrows suggestively.

"Now that I'm getting a better look at ya, where did all your cuts and scrapes go?" She totally ignored his Neanderthal comment, refusing to acknowledge how very *much* she liked. Strong curiosity played at the forefront of her mind. "I know you had injuries, and I know you don't heal that fast. Nobody does."

"I'm not sure what you're talking about. I think the blast has gotten to your head. I only had a couple of minor scrapes. Hey, I'm gonna take a shower if you're all done in there." He pushed past her without waiting for her to answer, and closed the door.

Chapter Five

*E*vening came while Nathanael showered, and Callie had grown antsy and hungry. Thank goodness for the Domino's Pizza joint right next to the hotel.

"Man! What is that awesome smell?" He stood in the bathroom doorway with a towel barely wrapped around his waist, and she forgot how to breathe. Not a scrap of fat lay on the valleys and planes of his bronzed chest, abs, and arms. His thighs were as thick as tree trunks, and she couldn't help but peruse the space in between, imagining just what lay behind Curtain Number One.

"Jesus! How about you save the strip routine for Vegas and go put some clothes on!" *Nice save, Callie-girl. Nice save.*

"What's the problem? You had a towel wrapped around you, and I had no complaints."

"My towel covered me, and you're a cad." She prayed the flush of heat throughout her body didn't show on her face, and grabbed hold of the dresser she'd leaned against. "Would ya take your clothes and your big, bad self into the bedroom and get dressed, please?" He started to release the towel. She covered her face in her hands. "The bedroom!"

"Only teasing." He chuckled and closed the French doors behind him.

What an egotistical ass he is, she thought. Just like Kemuel. *But it is a mighty fine ass at that.*

"Hey! Next time, use the other room if you want to wash up! It's got a perfectly good shower in it."

A few minutes later he came back out fully dressed in relaxed jeans and a tank top. "Safety and efficiency are crucial right now, so you're never gonna be that far from me. I asked you before about that awesome smell. Pizza?"

"Yes, Domino's is right next door. Don't be angry. I was starving and figured you were, too."

"Well, you should have waited for me. It's not safe for you to be out in public on your own right now. Did you use cash or charge?"

"Cash. I know better than to charge anything right now. It can be traced and found."

"I'm impressed you know anything about that." He grabbed a slice from the box and ate it in two bites, and took two more pieces with him to the couch. He pointed to the box. "Dig in, and let's talk."

Shit. Here we go. "Okay. What do you want to talk about?" He stopped chewing and gawked. "Oh, all right. You want me to spill." She took a deep cleansing breath and joined him. "Well, the short of it is that a long time ago, about twenty years now, thieves invaded our home and my father and mother were killed. The long of it? Men came looking for something my father owned and he wouldn't tell them where to find it. They got angry and killed them both in the foyer. I was upstairs at the time and hid in my secret hidey-hole I used for play. I couldn't identify who murdered my parents because they wore masks, so my lawyer eventually put me in a witness protection program of his own design and placed me in a new family until they could find the killers. I've lived my life since then as another person."

"I'm so sorry. So these killers have found you and are now after you for...?"

"For an item my father was going to have on display at his Curiosity Shop."

"And this item is what? A shrunken head? A monkey claw?"

"You're an ass." She punched him solidly in the shoulder, got up, and padded over to the hotel room window. "My father had wonderful pieces in his shop and traveled around the world to find them."

"Sorry, communication skills are not my best attribute when it comes to civilians. Out in the field, if you don't make jokes about everything, nothing is a joke and you wind up killing yourself. Consider my ass kicked. Come sit back down, would ya?" He patted the seat next to him. "So you've been able to stay hidden for how long again?"

"It's been about twenty years," she said, and sat on a chair instead. He whistled and raised an eyebrow. "Until stupid me impulsively clicked the contact button on a web page. Before I knew it, bam, a live-chat window opened up with someone ready to talk with me! Then, my lawyer, Mr. Watkins, left me a message on my answering machine telling me I'd been found and to run. Nathanael, I think something horrible's happened to him. He didn't sound good at all. The rest, you know. I thought you were the killers come to get me when you knocked on the door." She yawned and kneaded her shoulders.

"Where is this item now?"

"I don't know. It's hidden somewhere. I remember discussing it with Mr. Watkins, but you gotta know I was really messed up in the head. Most of that time is a blank to me now. He gave me an envelope with a note in it. He told me never to open it, to keep it in a locked box at all times. The paper has the location and directions on how to obtain the damn thing." She yawned again. "Whew, excuse me."

"No problem." He pressed on. "Where is, or was, your father's shop and what's its name?"

"Can't we finish this up in the morning? I'm exhausted and achy."

He scrubbed his face with his hands. "Just tell me the name of the shop and where it's located and we'll stop for now."

"Fine, you big brute!" She paused and took a breath to calm

her frustration. "It's called Murati's Curiosity shop now, and it's in Las Vegas. His shop, well, now my uncle's shop, is off the Strip. Now I'm not answering another question tonight. I'm going to bed. If you're not satisfied with my answers, you can leave, or stay. Your choice. If you're staying, I'll sleep under, you sleep over, and stay on your own side or I'll knee you in the balls. Understood?"

"I think I'll hang around a bit longer. We'll finish up in the morning. You can have the whole bed. I'll be up for a while working."

"Suit yourself." She stripped down the bed cover and began the ritual of wrapping herself up like a mummy with the sheets. She had done this bedtime ritual ever since "brother dear" first visited her, always with the hopes that he couldn't get through all of the many wrappings protecting her body all the way up to her neck; most of the time it worked. He'd get so fed up he'd curse and leave her room. To this day, it still comforted her being bound in such a way. She'd never make it easy for anyone, ever.

All Nathanael could do was stare in awe. *She looks like a freakin' mummy! Only someone who's been through a personal hell would require that sense of security and control. And Lord knows, I've seen plenty of men do the very same thing as she. What else besides her parents' murders is she hiding?*

He sat at the small table by the room's window and took out his phone. It would be best to start with a bit of research, but then, she'd never said her real name. He could locate the store easily enough, but without her real name, he wouldn't get much further, so tempting the fates and preparing for her razor-sharp retort, he asked. "Before you fall asleep there, what's your real name?"

"My real name?" Her eyes remained closed. "I...I don't think I can say it out loud. I whispered it just yesterday and nearly had a coronary." Her eyes opened. "I'm scared."

Nathanael approached the cocooned lump on the bed. He

knelt to caress her hair. "Why don't you whisper it to me, then? It's only you and me here, no one else. No one is gonna come charging in as soon as you say it. Okay? A small whisper for me, that's all." He watched as fear gripped her tighter than the bed sheets, and then subsided slowly as she nodded and closed her eyes.

"Come closer. Give me your ear," she croaked.

He leaned in so her lips nearly touched it.

"Ariana. Ariana Kupi."

No louder than a ghost's breath, she said her name, and he sensed years of pent-up anguish and terror. It pierced straight through to his soul, and he had no choice but to collect her in his arms and hold her. Hers trembled as she wrapped them around him.

"Shh. Shh. It's okay." He softly stroked her hair and murmured against her neck. How he knew what to do, he hadn't a clue. He'd never consoled or comforted a woman before. But it seemed right, and she smelled so good, he continued. "It's done. It's finished. Only you and I know. Rest now. I'll keep you safe."

She nodded against his chest and he laid her back down. She blinked up at him with eyes fringed by moist lashes. "Okay," she said, and sniffled, closing her eyes.

"Okay." He smiled and got up to return to the table. He had a name. And now, the researching could begin. Earlier, he had surreptitiously tried to trace her intent, tracking her by sense. When he put her backpack on the sofa, he'd stuck a hand inside to touch pieces of her clothing. Fear, anger, and a need to hide were strong threads throughout. There was no thought imprint about the sought-after piece itself or its whereabouts.

He sent a text to Gabriel Seeker, a Brethren Protector and information guru. If anyone could expose tightly guarded information, he could. Nathanael knew she had the Elixxir, but fiercely protected its identity. Smart girl. If she knew its true capabilities, and he believed she did, telling just anyone about it would put her safety at risk. Her parents were a prime example. But he needed her to trust him and tell him everything about it herself.

Was it really a need? No, he could find that flask without ever saying its name, without her sharing one more bit about it at this point. It was a want. He desperately wanted her to open up to him, to trust him implicitly. A very tall order, to be sure, looking at it from her standpoint. She'd always remained closed off from others, and now he knew why. But it stung to know that she closed herself off from him as well. Guilty by association. Kemuel screwed up and left a wake to follow. Add to that, killers hot on her trail and other childhood experiences that probably left her with emotional scars, and you got a person who wouldn't trust anyone.

He wanted to be that one person to break through all of that mess. Her situation had dredged up all sorts of memories of his own from his last black-ops' mission, where all of his team members had died. Since that devastating blow, he'd stopped believing others would ever trust him to lead a successful mission. So he'd quit and turned to bounty hunting instead, where he could work alone. Helping her could be his chance at redemption, his opportunity to show her—and prove to himself—how reliable he could be.

Furthermore, if she believed in the Elixxir's powers, then maybe he'd have a better shot at her believing in him and his true identity. He scratched his head. *Why? Why am I doing this? Why am I letting her get under my skin? She's nothing but trouble with a capital T. But those violet eyes. Mesmerizing, with a capital M. Ah! She hates me, and I don't need a woman in my life. It's too dangerous. I should just do my damn job. Find the Elixxir, get it, and go. Oh, and get the jerks that are after her. That would be a supreme pleasure.* His body shook with the thrill of an impending hunt.

Rustling of sheets broke through his musings. She turned over in her sleep, muttered something unintelligible, and settled back down. As much as he didn't want to leave her alone, he needed to do a little search-and-recovery over at the apartment complex.

He locked the hotel room up tight with the deadbolt and a chair wedged under the doorknob. He knew the adjoining room would come in handy, not just for protection, but as an easy way for him to get in and out without compromising security. Stepping out of the empty room and onto the second floor walkway, he saw not a soul in sight. Unfurling his wings, he flew off into the night, as silent as an unspoken thought.

ભ

Blackened bits of unidentifiable matter lay strewn about the parking lot in front of what used to be Callie's first floor garden apartment. In its place remained a black hole encompassing not just hers, but a few others as well. Nathanael waited silently in the trees overhead for the last of the gawkers to go home. It didn't take long. Well into the middle of the night, he floated down as close to the opening as possible and hid his wings away. The acrid stench of burnt, wet plastic and wood permeated his nostrils. As he looked around he could tell whoever did this used a combination of natural gas and spark to completely incinerate the place. The assholes didn't seem to care who they took down with her!

He scoured through the muck, looking for the lock box she had mentioned earlier. There were no more wall divisions so he couldn't tell where one room finished and another began. Crunching and sloshing through the charred remains of her life, he finally came upon a sizable metal box standing about two feet high and across. Bingo. He squatted to check it out. Thick black soot covered it, but beyond that, the thing remained intact....and opened. *Damn it! Nothing inside. Figures.* Whatever Gabriel uncovered in his search would be the only chance of finding the Elixxir now.

Something glinted at him out of the corner of his eye. He turned to his left and trudged over toward the back of the apartment. He bent over to find a two-inch silver key attached to a chain. Given the fact that other apartments had been burned, he couldn't be sure if it belonged to her or not. Pocketing it, he made a mental note to ask her about it in the morning. With nothing left to see, he flew away as silently as he had come.

 C3

Nathanael alighted by their hotel window and his supernatural hearing picked up on a distressed woman's voice. He immediately grabbed the Beretta from his boot. The voice sounded like Callie's for sure. He hadn't heard anyone else's coming from the room, but being in his line of work, you never could tell.

"I don't owe you anything, Dennis. Get off me. No...won't tell your parents.... I know I'm not your real sister. It doesn't matter! Please don't!"

With angelic speed, he entered their unoccupied room and burst through the adjoining door, ready to pummel the bastard that had found his way in. He aimed to the left and right and to the bed, fully expecting to see some thug accosting her. But she was alone. Her arms worked feverishly to remove invisible threats to her thighs as she tossed about, the terror in her voice escalating. He put the safety back on the gun and holstered it.

"Damn it," he muttered. He hurried over to the distraught woman and gently shook her shoulder. "Callie, wake up. You're dreaming." She carried on, yelling for Dennis to leave her alone. Telling him she was too young and asking how he could do this to her after everything she'd been through. She twisted herself into a frenzy, nearly falling off the bed. "Callie! Wake up!" He shook her harder. She jolted awake, flailing her arms about, slapping his chest in the process.

"What? What? Why are you waking me up?" She sat up and squeezed herself out of the sheet's wrappings like a snake shedding its skin. "What's going on? And where's your shirt?"

"You were having a nightmare and almost fell off the bed." He rubbed his stubbly cheeks and chose to ignore her last question. "You all right now? You wanna talk about it?"

She put her head in her hands as awareness washed over her face. "Shit," she muttered. "No. I don't want to talk about it."

"It might help." He reached out to her.

"Don't touch me. Just leave me alone, okay?" She got out of bed and scurried to the bathroom. Before he could blink, he heard the shower going.

He sighed and sat down on a chair. *Shit is right. Dennis must be the son from that family the lawyer placed her with. That son-of-a-bitch sexually assaulted her.* It explained so much. He heard her crying softly. Between the obvious post-traumatic stress and sexual abuse, he had no idea how she'd kept it as together as she had. Over his many centuries in the military and bounty hunting, he'd seen it all. Stronger men had been brought down by less. So she tucked herself into bed funny and talked in her sleep. She was abrasive and secretive. He could get past those walls, given enough time and some advice from Emma D'Angelo. She would know how to reach her. Heck, the Great Savior Mother could even heal her. He made another mental note to call Emma in the morning.

The shower stopped. Curtain hooks scraped and screeched across the shower rod. A few minutes later, Callie emerged, rubbing her hair with a towel. She wouldn't look at him. She wore her boxer shorts and tank top again, giving him a perfect view of bright red skin that accentuated the lingering cuts and scrapes earned earlier in the evening. She'd scrubbed herself raw.

"All better now?"

"Yeah, tons." She sneered and sat on the bed. She looked at him for the briefest of moments and then down at her hands, using her wet hair as a curtain. "Listen, I'm really uncomfortable now, here, with you having seen and heard.... It happens sometimes, my nightmares."

"Hey, we all have crap to deal with from our past. Even from our present. It's nothing to be ashamed of. You've had a hell of a couple of days here that I'm sure played a big part in bringing them out. I can't unhear what I've heard, though. So you'll have to get past it." He leaned forward in his chair, forearms resting on his knees. "Tell me, is this Dennis anywhere in your life now?"

She looked up at him, shamefaced. "I reported him to the police and he got seven years in jail. He was released, but I know he's had some run-ins with the law since. So no, no he's not a part of my life, except in my nightmares. He doesn't seem to want to let me go. As much as I try, he comes back every now and again to terrorize me like he used to."

"Do you usually scrub yourself raw in the shower like you did just now?"

She looked at her legs and arms and started to cry. "I can feel his hands on me. Still. Every time. When I wake up from one of these, I still feel his punishing touch. If I scrub hard enough, the pain numbs my skin." She wiped her tears with the towel and shook her head. "Oh, this has so not been a good day for me."

Nathanael knew she'd probably throw a fit, but he dared to do what his heart wanted him to do and his conscience screamed against. He sat down next to her, and putting his arm around her shoulder, pulled her in close. Ready for a slew of curses and yelling, he winced, but they never came. Instead, he felt her arm loop around his waist and her head fell against his chest.

"You know, if you tell me where he lives, I can beat him up for you." She tittered softly. "Or I could have him thrown in jail again on some trumped-up charges so he can be some inmate's bitch for a night." She slapped him lightly on his stomach.

"You'd do that for me?" She leaned her head back so she could see his face. He nodded. "Okay, you're not an ass anymore."

"Oh good, because that was really bothering me all day. I don't mind being called a piece of ass, but plain old ass just makes me sad." He winked. "Hey, slide back on the bed. I'm gonna show you how to sleep soundly and comfortably without wrapping yourself up like a mummy."

She looked dubious but complied with his demands. He lay down next to her and gathered her over to him, moving so fast she didn't have time to complain. At first, her body went rigid and tensed against his. "Nothing like a heartbeat's rhythm to relax you. Now settle in, take a few deep breaths, and close your eyes. I'm here, and you are safe. Think sweet thoughts like puppies or kittens or whatever you girls think is sweet." He didn't know what to say anymore, so he went for touch instead. *If only I had a Protector's skills of comforting and bringing peace, this would go a lot easier. My strength and cunning are all I got.* He smoothed his hand against her damp hair and then stopped to massage her head lightly. Her body loosened. She groaned and snuggled closer. He smiled. *Maybe I don't need Emma's help after all. I must be a natural.*

He waited until her breathing became even and regular.

Nah, just damn lucky.

Chapter Six

Callie decided that on her list of must-haves should be one of those sound machines with a heartbeat on it. Nathanael's real heartbeat, slow and steady, was the perfect remedy to her restless sleep and she could very easily get used to hearing it every night. She smiled. *Get a load of you! Going soft on him, are we? Could it have anything to do with how he said he could beat up Dennis for you, or is it his luscious, half-naked body fitting perfectly next to yours? Or could it be the way he said he'd keep you safe? Check off all of the above.*

Kemuel never said stuff like that to her. No, he was a total lunkhead. A sexy and funny lunkhead, but clueless in the women department. He may have been good for many a romp in bed, but long, deep conversations weren't his forte. Then again, she hadn't wanted that at the time, either. She'd wanted an escape from her sorry excuse of a life. In the end, if she analyzed their relationship, he couldn't possibly have been the right one for her. Nope. Not at all.

Nathanael isn't either, Callie-girl. She had to remember she'd sworn off men completely. Abstaining from all relationships until she got her shit together took top billing in her book. Maybe softening a little toward him would be harmless to her goal. He had been super nice and willing to help fight off the bad guys and find the Elixxir. She frowned slightly against his chest. *Why, I wonder? What's in it for him?* Another puzzle to solve another day. She set it aside and sank in deeper to his body, drifting off to sleep.

ᚼ

Nathanael watched as Gabriel swooped down from the sky to land before him on the second floor walkway, and shook his hand. "Hey, Brother, thanks for coming. How are ya?"

"I'm good, I'm good." He retracted his wings and dug into the back pocket of his leather pants. "Mission accomplished. Ariana Kupi is the daughter of the slain Joseph and Celeste Kupi. She went dark twenty years ago, and for all intents and purposes, died, too. Trail ends. Her father was partners with one Edward Murati of Las Vegas, Nevada. They owned Kupi and Murati's Curiosity Shop. I found some scary tidbits on the now sole owner of the store."

"Do tell."

"Well, first of all, his shop was a suspected front for drug dealing."

"You're kidding."

"Nope. I checked his financials. He should barely be making ends meet, given profit/loss statements. But when I dug deeper, I found out he lives in a multimillion-dollar mansion, and he's got a personal jet to his name, as well, that takes him to Tahiti several times a year. I'm still trying to locate precisely where he goes. I'll get back to you on that."

"So he's rich. Where's the hard evidence about drugs? They were real close. She called him uncle, you know. I gotta tread carefully and have undisputable proof that he's into illegal stuff before I go telling her anything."

"Is this file hard enough evidence for ya?" Gabriel passed a manila folder to him. "Don't ask me where I got it. I'd have to kill ya." He chuckled.

"Give me your short version. It'll be just as thorough, I'm sure."

"He's been investigated in the past, charged numerous times for dealing cocaine and ecstasy, but none of the charges stuck. They were all mysteriously dropped each time."

"Interesting. He's got someone high up in his pocket. Wonder if he involved her father as well before he and his wife were murdered?"

"The first charge goes back a long ways, about twenty years ago."

"Hmmm. Her parents were murdered twenty years ago." He pinched the bridge of his nose and closed his eyes briefly. "All right, so we got a no-good uncle running her father's old shop as a front for drugs. Lovely. Hey, would you take a look at this while you're here? It's a key I found looking through the burnt remains of her apartment. What's it go to? Do you know?"

Nathanael handed over the key he'd been fumbling with since they'd begun talking, and waited patiently while watching Gabriel turn it over and over in his hands.

"Hmm. It looks to me to be a key to a locker in a bus station. See how it says B54 on this side?" Gabriel pointed to the engraving. "That tells you that it's in Section B, locker number 54. But to what specific station, I haven't a clue. Instincts tell me, though, if it's hers, and you find the locker to that key, you'll find yourself with a whole bunch of answers. How is she?"

"Messed up, man. Still very guarded. PTSD has a strong hold on her, but I'm wearing her down." He smirked. "I thought I'd be able to get my hands on that Elixxir, no problem, but she has no idea where it is."

"Do what you can with her until Raphael and Emma are available to help. I gotta go, but if you need anything else, I'm free and so are Michael, Urie, and Kemuel."

"Uh yeah, well, Kemuel's gonna have to stay far away from this mission. Suffice it to say, he and Callie should not be in the same with room with each other for a good long while."

"Okay, not gonna ask. Don't want to know. Oh, hey! I almost forgot. E.L. says he's got an upgrade for you Warriors to check out and use from here on out. He's ramped up your shielding capabilities to transparent. Now you can shield your threaded signature and your appearance. There's nothing better than hearing the word 'upgrade' in my world, so you're freakin' lucky. Call me, bro." Gabriel stood, released his wings, and flew off into the purple sky. Dawn was coming, and with it a whole host of questions for one complicated woman.

Nathanael trudged back into the room, tossing the key about in his hand. His senses revealed no more about it. Not the slightest thread of intent or emotion remained. He'd have to rely on Callie to offer up any additional information. The rhythmic rise and fall of her body told him the enigmatic woman still lay sleeping. He'd have to wake her up soon if they were going to make decisions on what to do next. Sitting on a chair, he stared at her back, trying to wrap his head around a plan percolating in his mind.

"Stop staring. You're creeping me out."

He laughed. "I didn't think you were awake. How do you know I'm looking at you? You're not even facing my direction."

"I don't. You just confirmed my suspicions. Kemuel always watched me sleep." She turned over and glared at him. "I don't know what it is about you guys. You seem to have an aversion to sleeping or something."

"We need to talk about what we're doing today," he said, diverting her attention to a more suitable topic.

She leaned up on her elbow and sighed. "I think all signs lead to Vegas." He raised a brow in surprise. "I think we need to go there. I can't let these killers get their hands on what's mine. And what's mine has to be there somewhere. Maybe you, being all Brethren Security, black ops, and bounty hunter-ish, can do what the cops haven't been able to do in twenty years. Catch the assholes who killed my parents. I'm not sure, though, where to start once we're there."

"Why don't you start with this?" He took the locker key from his pocket and poured the chain into her palm.

"What?"

"I don't know. Why don't you tell me?" He sat back and

folded his hands on his lap.

"Well, it's a key, of course." She put it around her neck and tucked it under her tank top.

He leaned in. "Apparently it's yours."

"Yes, it's mine. Where did you find it?"

"Back at your apartment, or what used to be your apartment. What does it open?"

"I don't know, actually. My father gave it to me when I was a little girl and told me it was the key to his heart. I used to wear it all the time. I wasn't supposed to keep anything from my former life, but I couldn't help it. I had to have something tangible from my parents, so I hid it no matter where I lived. I should thank you for finding it." She smiled.

"You're welcome. I think it's an important piece to all of this. Try to remember. Did your dad ever take you to a bus station when you were a little girl and use the key?"

She closed her eyes and her brow furrowed. After a few moments, she opened them. "I can't remember. I don't know." Bristling, she pushed the sheets to the side, crawled over to her backpack, and then sifted through a mound of clothes, ultimately pulling out a fresh pair of shorts and a T-shirt. "I'll only be a couple minutes, and then we can go."

Yeah, and then I can knock the wall down you built up.

∞

Callie's skin sizzled like potato chips in a convection oven. Swirling waves of heat punished every pore, wrung out precious drops of moisture from her body, and quickly whisked it away. They'd been riding on his Harley, beating up the road, for a couple of hours now. Surely she'd lost a good twenty pounds in water weight, and her butt needed a break desperately. She tapped him on the shoulder and shouted in his ear.

"Can we stop? Butt's killing me!"

He nodded and pointed to an approaching sign that said, "Rest Stop—10 miles."

Oh, thank the dear Lord! She gingerly stood, using the foot pegs to stretch a little bit, and repositioned herself on the joke of a passenger seat. It would be ten more miles of nothing better to do than beat herself up for her predicament.

"If only" kept cropping up in her brain. If only she hadn't pushed the damned computer key, she wouldn't be in this mess. If only she hadn't had that infernal nightmare in front of Nathanael, he wouldn't be acting all nice and behaving like a man who cared. If only she wasn't starting to have feelings for the jerk, this ride would be so much easier! Four more hours she had left to endure his masculine scent assaulting her hormones, his power undulating beneath her hands, and his body speaking naughty things to hers. *I am such a loser! I decide to swear off men and what do I do with the first one who shows the least bit of kindness? I get all hot and bothered by him! I need off this bike!*

Before she realized it, he had slowed down and veered off the road to the rest stop. "Why don't you take a walk around for a few minutes? I'll go and get us something to eat and drink."

She grunted as she lifted her weary body off the motorcycle. "Sounds like a plan. I'm gonna go to the restroom. Would ya get me the largest bag of Corn Nuts you can find, and a bottle of water, please?"

"Sure thing." He got off his bike, showing no signs of fatigue whatsoever. Too tired to be pissed, she shuffled over to the bathrooms at the side of the Quickmart.

"Ten dollars regular on number eleven." Nathanael loaded up the counter with Callie's requests and his own Coke and slice of pizza. The woman gave him the once-over multiple times, and he considered asking *her* for payment for services rendered.

"That'll be eighteen dollars, seventy-five cents."

He fished a fifty-dollar bill out of his wallet and handed it to her. Funny how she didn't scrutinize that as well as she did him. He chuckled to himself. After receiving his change and another flagrant bit of ogling, he made his way out the door, only to be slammed in the face with the sexiest view to hit his eyes in a long time. Callie stalked over to the bike, hips swishing side to side and hair dripping wet, leaving rivulets running down her arms and back. He had the sudden urge to follow those lines with his tongue.

As the door swung closed, it hit him in the ass, jarring him from his less-than-angelic thoughts. Something else did as well. The sense of fear and annoyance. It emanated from the sexy redhead, and he immediately saw why. A huge, grimy man had shuffled over to her and was making lewd comments and propositions. *And I'm different from him, how? Oh right, at least I keep my depraved thoughts to myself!* He sighed and shook his head, carefully putting the food and drink on the narrow sidewalk. Cracking his knuckles and angling his neck from side to side, he lumbered over to the escalating scene.

Callie's fear had manifested itself into a flurry of colorful curses and a string of suggestions as to what would happen should the man even attempt to touch her, but he knew it was a cover. He sensed the terror she kept in check, and gave her bonus points for bravado. The derelict simply laughed and took a menacing step toward her. Nathanael's shadow loomed large over the smelly, disheveled pig as he closed in as well. *Showtime....*

"All right, buddy, why don't you move on now? The lady's not interested."

"I'm just showing her my appreciation for her lusty appearance, is all. Can't a man compliment a lady anymore these days? Jeee-zus! And who the hell are you to butt into our business anyways? She's warming up to me, and you have to put your nose in it."

"I'm her guardian angel, shit-for-brains. So move on or I'm gonna have to get ugly on your ass."

"Ha! Right! Not likely when I have this." Quick as a blink, he pulled out a Glock from his waistband and pointed it at Callie. "Now, you're gonna leave us alone, boy, to finish our business. Understand?"

She'd moved closer to him throughout the exchange, but not close enough to be shielded. Now frozen where she stood, her eyes widened and fear bloomed on her face. A thrum of energy coursed through his body as this imbecile ignited his anger, and he smelled the putrescence of evil wafting across the expanse between them. Vibrations of latent power shivered across his skin as the anticipation built.

What a puny attempt at intimidation! The thug would be no match for his angelic speed and skills. Besides, with security cameras watching their every move, he knew he had to dispatch him quickly. Like a rush of wind, Nathanael flew over and knocked the gun clear out of the man's hand. He figured, from the man's cries, he'd broken bones in the process. Then he punched him in the gut for good measure. Amidst shrieks, curses, and protests, he proceeded to pick him up, walk over to the Dumpster, and throw him in with a grunt and growl of his own. He collected the piece, winked at Callie, who blinked at him, speechless, and returned to the convenience store. By the time he reached the clerk, the initial adrenaline rush had receded a bit.

"Miss, there's a man in your Dumpster at the moment. I relieved him of this here weapon he chose to point at my lady friend." He laid it down on the rubber mat by the cash register. "I suggest you call the police. Have a nice day." He turned his back on the second woman he'd rendered speechless that day, and walked out. With food and drink back in his hands, he found Callie'd taken up residence on the back of his bike.

"Water and the largest bag of Corn Nuts I could buy." He extended the offerings to her. She looked at them and took them without comment. "You did real good back there, Red. Said some curses I didn't even know." He chuckled.

"Can we go, please?" She frowned and took a long swig from her bottle of water.

He gave her back a pat and she flinched. "Hey, you gotta shake it off, now. Nothing bad happened. I told you I'd protect you."

"Men are assholes, through and through. Present company not included. But there's still time for you to fuck that up, too. I'm not hungry anymore. Can we please go?"

"All righty, then. There's my snarky girl!" He swallowed down the slice of pizza in three easy bites and took a long swig of his Coke.

He got on his bike and started the engine. Not more than five minutes down the road, she tapped him on his shoulder and pointed for him to pull over onto the side of the road. He immediately did so.

"What's up?" Callie flew off the bike and paced back and forth. "Something wrong with your seat? Got a cramp?"

She stopped in front of him and waved his questions off. "No, my seat is fine, and I don't have a cramp. I have a question."

"You had me stop for a question? You couldn't wait until we arrived in Las Vegas?"

Wagging a finger, she looked him square in the eye. "How did you do it?"

"How did I do what?"

"How did you get to that guy so fast and remove the gun? One minute you're over here," she said, gesturing to her left. "And then you're on top of the guy, batting the gun away. Plus, he's huge and you picked him up like he was a feather. I want answers, Nate. No normal guy can do what you did today. And your scratches from the blast yesterday, gone. Curiosities are starting to pile up. I don't like curiosities. I'm not going another mile with you until you give me some answers." She folded her arms over her chest and planted her feet on the solid ground.

She's on to me, damn it. I can't lie, so what on earth am I going to say?

"Well, if you really must know, then I'll tell you. But it's gotta be a secret kept between us. No one must know."

"Oh, great. You know what? I know what you're gonna say, and damn it. It's so bad for you. Steroids are not the answer, Nate."

He thought about correcting her assumption, but stopped himself just in time. Hell, he didn't say it, and if he didn't agree with her, he still wasn't lying. Technically.

"What gave you that impression?" He kicked at some dirt and looked down for an added dramatic effect.

She scoffed and waved her hands madly about as she circled around him. "Let's see, you're huge, for one thing. All those muscles are fighting to burst out of your skin! You're super-fast. I mean, you were on that Neanderthal in a flash, Nate. You're super strong to lift and carry him the way you did. Unreal! Oh, and let me not forget the crazed look you had in your eyes. They nearly glowed! That was one crazy 'roid look if I ever saw one." She shook her head.

"Well," he said, smacking his hands together. "Now that we have that settled, shall we get going so we can make Las Vegas before it gets dark?" He'd been a lucky little shit because that could have exploded in his face. He smiled, mounted the bike, and motioned for her to get back on.

She did, and poked his shoulder. "Get off the 'roids, Nate. They're gonna kill ya. Ready when you are."

Chapter Seven

Callie leaned against the hotel balcony railing, looking out onto the Las Vegas Strip. They'd arrived at the Tropicana a couple of hours ago, and she couldn't be more melancholy. Bright lights had begun to show their glimmer, but vague childhood memories flitted in and out of her mind, obscuring her view. She imagined herself a wee bit of a thing, holding hands with her father and mother, walking down the sidewalk, and being frightened. She hated the greasy-looking men who got in people's faces and handed out cards of nearly naked women. And the women, well, some of them were pretty enough, but most of them were scary ugly and wore clothes two sizes too small.

She hadn't remembered much, but one thing she did recall quite clearly. She hated Las Vegas.

"I just got off the phone with the front desk. A room opened up with two queen beds in it. They're sending up our keys right now." Nathanael had come outside, and she hadn't even noticed. Turning her back on the Strip, she focused on the mammoth individual standing before her. He took up all the available space out on the tiny bit of a landing, and then some.

"Okay, that's great. Thanks. I didn't mean to make a stink about it when we arrived, but I thought it would be better to have two beds since I'm such a restless sleeper."

He laughed. "Well, your stink has sent us to the penthouse level, so I should be thanking you."

"Ooh, the penthouse level. How glamorous. Maybe there'll be more room on that balcony." She coughed and maneuvered around him, trying her best not to make contact with his body as she went back into the room. The trip had given her plenty of touchy-feely time to last her quite a while. At the moment, she was having a heck of a time trying to forget the way his body had kissed and caressed hers with every bump and curve in the road. The way it vibrated in tune with the Harley's powerful engine.

He sniffed his armpits. "Do I offend?"

"What?" She laughed nervously. "No."

"Then I must have cooties." He raised an eyebrow.

"Oh, stop! I know what you're getting at. I'm trying to stay away from you because your big, manly body has battered mine all day long on that bike. One more touch and someone's gonna call the police for domestic violence due to all the bruising on my skin." She hurried through the sliding glass door and went straight into the bathroom. She could still hear his roar of laughter. *Asshole! Hot, sexy, freakin' asshole!* She looked at her scowl in the mirror and started laughing, too. *I'm an idiot. Time for a cold shower and a new frame of mind.* She had to find that Elixxir before the bad guys did. There could be no other scenario. If only she could remember more about where the Elixxir might be. She closed her eyes and tried to reach back to a place she never truthfully wanted to return to again. The dark place in time when her privileged life turned into an endless nightmare. She breathed deeply and held on to the sink for support. But it was of no use. The wall her fragile mind had erected proved too strong to let her simply move it aside after so much time had passed.

A light rap on the bathroom door teased her back to the present. "Callie, our keys are here. Time to go."

She unclenched her fingers from their death grip. *Damn it. It didn't work.* "Okay, I'm coming."

Nathanael had both of their bags slung over his shoulder,

and he held the room's door open. She nodded as she went by him and into the hall. Walking the length of it in silence, she nibbled a fingernail, not sparing a glance over at him as they stepped into the elevator and rode it to the penthouse floor.

"Mighty quiet over there. What's up?" He nudged her arm and she glared back.

"Nothing's necessarily up, Nate. I'm just having a quiet moment. That's all."

"Oh, really?" He raised a brow and smirked.

"Oh, all right. Might as well tell you since you'll pester it out of me eventually. In the bathroom, I tried remembering back to...that time long ago. The time I seem to have blocked. And, well, it's useless. I still can't remember a damn thing. That part of my life seems closed off to me forever. So, I don't have a clue as to how we are going to continue on this crazy quest."

"Don't worry, I have a plan." He rubbed her back. "The key is the first step. There's a bus station where I think it's probably from." The elevator door opened. As they exited and looked at the sign on the wall to find their room number, he continued. "You're going to stay here while I check it out."

She stopped short. "Oh no, I'm not." She crossed her arms. "You're not getting this key and going anywhere without me. Don't even think about arguing."

"Do you have any idea how rough a neighborhood this bus station is in? It's like a war zone! No one in their right mind would venture there. I'm not taking you, so forget it."

"Then you can forget about me giving you the key." She turned and stalked on down the hall.

"Uh, you're going the wrong way. Our room is over here." He pointed behind him. "So much for your dramatic exit, huh?" He laughed and flashed his perfectly white teeth as she huffed past him.

"Smartass...." she grumbled. "You're not getting it unless I go with. Case closed."

She stood, a silent statue by their door, while he put the card in the lock, pushed the door open, and waved her in.

He swore under his breath. "If you're coming with me, then you'll need to put on different clothes. Something much less revealing. I know I'm a big, strong man, but even I have my limits when it comes to warding off dangerous people. Do you have anything in here?" He dropped her bag on one of the queen-sized beds. And he did have his limits, probably. He just hadn't reached them yet.

"I have shorts and tank tops. Everything else is gone."

"Time to shop, then." He dug into his pocket. "Here, take this. We're going to get you some jeans, looser fitting ones, and a few baggy T-shirts." She looked at his fistful of bills. "Listen, you can't use your credit card, and whatever cash you do have, I want you to have for emergencies only. Oh, and since you can't use your phone anymore, let's get you a burner phone."

"A burner phone?"

"Yes, a throw-away, untraceable."

"Oh, okay. Thanks, that makes a lot of sense."

"Yeah, well I do make sense every so often. Get used to it." She snorted, grabbed the money, and started to leave. "Hey, wait! Here's your room key, and you don't get beyond five feet from me, you hear?"

She took the key from his offered hand and shoved it in her bag. "Trying on clothes should be quite interesting then." She winked and sashayed out.

Oh, she's asking for it! Truth be told, the loose-fitting clothes were as much for his sake as for her safety. If he had to see her voluptuously kick-ass body in her skimpy shorts and tank top much longer, he might very well explode from carnal need. If only she wouldn't argue so much, she'd be perfect! He did enjoy the verbal sparring, sometimes. Yeah, the banter teased his fun side, but the obstinacy was getting tiresome. He'd have to do something about that or he'd find this mission taking twice as long to accomplish. Holstering his Beretta, and shielding it against detection, he grabbed his leather duster and left the room.

"Nathanael?"

Her worried voice called to him. Well, as much as she was stubborn, he believed she was also, at times, still a young girl trapped in her woman's body.

He smiled and squeezed her arm gently. "Right behind ya. Don't worry."

ⱷ

"They don't make baggy jeans anymore, Nate! Now come on—" Callie flew her hands up. "This is the tenth pair I've tried on. I'm picking one and taking it. Enough is enough. It'll be midnight before we make it to the station at the rate we're going."

"Then I'll get you a bigger size and a belt. That'll make them baggy and saggy. Perfect for blending. What size are you?" She gave him a look of death. "What? Just tell me so I can get you a bigger size. I promise I won't tell anyone." She raised six fingers. He turned and went to the jeans rack to pick out the larger size.

"Here, try these on."

She sighed and took the pair into the dressing room. When she came out she looked miserable. He smiled. "See, that's what I'm talking about."

"Great, glad you're happy to see me looking so frumpy."

She'd pouted so adorably, it took him by surprise. She trudged back into the dressing room. He couldn't help himself, and took a quick look around. Seeing no attendants nearby at the moment, his adventurous side had to follow. He moved the dressing room curtain aside and stepped in, drawing it back around him for privacy.

"Hey!" She swung around and whispered vehemently. "What do you think you're doing?"

He towered over her, backing her up against the mirror and put one hand on either side of her head. Careful to leave only enough space so their bodies wouldn't touch, he looked her straight in the eyes and whispered back. "For your information, you would look sexy as hell in a potato sack, and still do in those jeans." He winked and left as her jaw dropped.

What the hell was that all about? Did he do what I think he did? Damn. The man just came on to me! Anger warred with arousal as she tore the tags off her new clothes and collected her things from the bench. She whipped the curtain open and stormed out toward the cashier's counter where the insufferable oaf leaned nonchalantly.

She gave the tags to the salesgirl, smiled, and turned to him, speaking in a hushed but intense voice. "You and I are gonna have words when I'm done here." She heard him snort as she turned back to the girl and smiled, paying for her clothes, but paying him no mind. Grabbing the plastic bag with a couple pairs of skinny jeans and her own shorts and top inside, she marched past Nathanael and out the door.

"Have a great night!" an oblivious saleswoman called out to her. She waved her off with a grunt and a "Whatever."

She watched as the overly-confident Neanderthal sauntered out of the store and headed straight over to her. Even though they were outside, he seemed to take up all the usable space in the immediate vicinity.

"You got words for me, Red?"

"I got plenty for you, Nate." She poked his chest, trying to push him back a bit. "Wanna hear some? How about, you're a jerk for walking into my dressing room without permission? How about, what the hell was that back there, asking my dress size and calling me sexy as hell? How about—"

Her next words were gobbled up by a hot, urgent mouth pressed against her own. Strong hands held her shoulders, guiding her closer to his body as he deepened his assault on her lips. At first, she didn't know what to do. He'd shocked the hell out of her with his aggression. She couldn't help noticing some of her protective walls had been torn asunder, and well-guarded ramparts were crumbling. Eyes that at first had flown open wide were now fluttering closed as her mind claimed temporary insanity.

She gave in. Her hands crawled up his stomach to his chest and on up to his face, where she held him and retaliated with her own brand of attack. Their tongues, like swords, thrust and parried while she let her hands roam onward through his thicket of wavy black hair.

A horn blared, bringing her back to reality and the cracked sidewalk where she stood, with lips being molested by a beautifully dangerous man. *Not again! I won't fall for another employee of Brethren Security!* She ripped herself away and stepped back. Breathing heavily, she shot him a look she hoped would convey death if he so much as moved an inch toward her. In case he wasn't good at reading signals, she raised her hands to stop any forward advance. To his credit, he looked possibly even more stunned than she, and stood his ground.

"I...I'm sorry. First, you were looking all pouty, and then you were in my face all angry, and I don't know what came over me." He raked a hand through his hair.

"You don't know? Well, I'd hate to see what you'd do when you do have your wits about you." She shook her head. "Nate, I can't...we can't...."

"I know. I know. You don't have to spell it out for me. Come on, let's go to the bus station and try to forget what just happened. Let's do what we came here to do."

"Right. That's all I want. And to stay alive."

Chapter Eight

Nathanael pulled the Harley into a parking space close to the entrance of the bus terminal. He tapped her knee, signaling her to get off, and grabbed her hand possessively, letting anyone who cared to know that she was his property. She flinched at first, but when he gave her his go-along–with-me-or-else look, she seemed to get the hint.

As they entered the station, they squeezed through a wall of unsavory people. His senses were bombarded by the flickering fluorescent lighting and an acrid odor of urine and cleaning fluid. Immediately, he raised his olfactory shields at the offense. Looking over at Callie, he saw her grimacing slightly. Humans were lucky sometimes not have the ultra-keen senses of the immortals.

Taking a visual sweep of the open area, he noticed a lull in activity. It was known to be a busy hub, but only a few people were in line at the ticket counter in front of them. A few others were seated on worn, plastic chairs, luggage tightly gripped in hand. A group of teenagers stood off to the side, huddled in a corner, looking over their shoulders. Probably a drug exchange going down. Not his problem at the moment. He spotted a wall of lockers to his right, floor to near-ceiling, rusty and deteriorated.

"Over there. The lockers." He pointed to them for Callie.

"I see. Well, guess we should go take a peek and then, I don't know how many showers it's gonna take for me to feel clean again."

"I agree. Come on."

They hurried over and scanned the numbers on the locker doors until they found the B section and locker 34, sitting innocuously in between 33 and 35. Did he really expect it would be painted bright red with neon arrow signs pointing to it? She glanced at him, nibbled her lower lip, and slowly took the key from around her neck.

"I don't mind saying I'm scared."

"Want me to open it for you?"

"No, no. I'll do it. I just have no idea what we're going to find." She extended a trembling hand and tried her key in the lock. It shook so much she took her other hand to steady herself. "Damn it," she muttered.

"Here, no sense in going crazy. Let me." He gentled the key from her hand, pushed it in the lock, and turned. It clicked open.

The hinges whined mercilessly as he opened the door. "God, that's dreadful!" She put her fingers in her ears.

"What have we here?"

"What is it? She leaned against him, trying to get a peek as he reached in and retrieved a manila envelope.

He turned it over in his hands, checking it out. His angel warrior senses sought out any lingering traces of intent or motive from the last person who held it. No matter how long it'd been around, there could still be a thread or two he could exploit to their benefit. "Look. It says, *In case of emergency.*"

"Well. I'd say this is one heck of an emergency. Wouldn't you?"

"Yeah. Come on." Senses told him a male had left this envelope. Sadness and trepidation were the last emotions exuded by him. Her father perhaps? More than likely. He closed the locker door, took her hand once again, and proceeded to walk out the exit. "Let's get outta here and back to the safety of our room."

"No argument from me." He stopped short and turned to her.

"Really? That's a first. Thank you." He laughed and continued on.

She swatted his arm playfully. "Oh, shut up."

"Crap," he muttered.

"What?" Alarm sounded in her voice.

"We got company at the bike. Damn it." He knew it had been too good to be true. Their trip had gone far too smoothly up to this point. He didn't want to make another scene in front of her. She already suspected something from the last scuffle. But these guys weren't admiring the bike. His supernatural hearing picked up midway through their conversation. They were discussing prices for parts.

"Maybe they're simply talking about its finer qualities, showing some appreciation for its beauty. They'll move on when we get close."

"Doubt it. All right, do exactly as I say." He nudged her forward, adrenaline seeping into his bloodstream, hoping his sheer size would be intimidating enough to shoo them away. "Hey, gentlemen. Excuse us, but we've gotta be going."

All four men turned, and in unison their eyes flashed a brilliant red. *Damn it all! They* would *have to be some of Satan's minions.* He hoped Callie hadn't seen it, but her immediate death grip on his arm told him otherwise.

One of the delinquents stepped forward, moving his shirttail aside like a curtain to display a gun in his waistband. "Gonna have to take the bus home, asshole. This here bike now belongs to us." The other three joined him in creating a wall of thugs possessed by evil.

He passed her the envelope and patted her hands without shifting his glance. "Go back in the terminal, would you, darlin'?" He quickly peeled her fingers off his arm and shoved her behind him. She stumbled and then scurried away from the scene. "Now I can't do that. You see, that would be letting you all win. And I just can't let that happen." He moved his hands to his waist and flashed his own piece. If they wanted a fight, he'd sure as hell give them one they'd remember, Brethren style.

"You're one stupid fuck. There ain't no way you're gonna get out of this now."

"Bring it on, feces." He spat on the ground and beckoned them with a flick of his hands.

The four charged him with all the finesse of roosters in a cockfight. As one came close to peck at him with a knife, he swatted it away and landed an uppercut on the guy's jaw. He roundhouse-kicked another, throwing him into a third guy, and finally landed a left hook on the last man standing. All in a matter of ten seconds. His entire body shook with a mixture of dark and warrior energy as he loomed over their still bodies, lying strewn on the ground. Blood shushed through his heart at a rapid pace and he saw nothing but red before his eyes. He heard scuffling behind him and turned blindly, ready to knock out the next sorry soul, and snarled.

"Whoa! Whoa! It's me, Nathanael! Stop!"

A familiar voice burst through his mania and got hold of his soul, bringing him down from his violent high. Red spots faded before him and in their place stood a wide-eyed woman. Breathing heavily, he looked around and found four men unconscious on the ground. He turned back to the woman. He shook his head. What more would he have done had she not been there and called his name?

"Callie."

"Yes, it's me. Let's get out of here before the cops show up. Can you drive?"

"Yeah," he said absently. As he hopped on the bike, instincts took hold—*turn on the ignition, pull in the clutch, push the start button, put it in gear, let out the clutch, twist the throttle, and race out of here like a bat out of hell.*

The rumble of the engine did nothing to soothe him back down to a calmer, normal state. He craved a more violent release than what those sorry excuses for possessed humans had dealt him. No, they were a mere appetizer. He was all worked up and had no place to spend it. He had to get her back to their room and then head straight for the hotel's gym to release the pent-up energy. If she let him back into the room, it'd be a miracle.

Oh, my freakin' God! Who...what in God's name were those guys? And steroids couldn't possibly make Nathanael react so quickly. So what the hell is up with him? Callie white-knuckled the strap of her seat, not wanting to touch his body on the trip home. He'd frightened her, although he hadn't hurt her. He'd stopped as soon as he heard her voice. That proved interesting and piqued her curiosity even more.

Who was this man who had swooped into her life and promised to help her? A bounty hunter with a lust for violence, to be sure. Did she really want to be entangled with him given all the turmoil right now? A loose cannon could be her demise. What to do? What to do?

The sudden stillness, rather than vibration, roused her from her musings. They were back at their hotel, and not quite sure what to do next, she remained sitting, staring off into nowhere.

"We're here, you know. You can get up. I'm sure you're interested in seeing what's inside here." He waved the envelope in front of her.

"I am. But what I'm *more* curious about at the moment, Nathanael," she said while crossing her arms over her chest, "is what was wrong with those guys back there, and what exactly is going on with you." Being a pro at hiding fear behind bravado came in handy now. He shuffled his feet awkwardly and frowned while rubbing his chin with his hand.

And he remained silent.

"Well? You obviously know something and you're not telling me. We don't go one step further in this quest until you tell me what's happening here. Who are those freakish guys with the wacked-out eyes? And who are you, really?"

"Can we take this inside? I really don't want to do this in public."

"Fine. Let's go."

Shit. Why can't anything be simple? Why did I have to be so God-damned observant and see those flaming red eyes?

She stomped past him and through the sliding-glass doors, waving off a too-friendly doorman. The elevator ride lasted an eternity. Callie chose to brood while he refused to speak or even look at her.

What is that man thinking? Oh! He's insufferable!

She had her key out, ready to open the door before he could, and barreled through. Heading straight for a chair by the window, she tried to calm the growing trepidation inside as she sat down.

"Okay, mister, something really freaky is going on and it's time you let me in on it."

He kneeled, steadied her shaking knees, and took her trembling hands in his. Her fear and a desire to flee permeated his senses the longer he held them, yet she didn't move. Looking at Callie with all the seriousness this moment required, he opened up to her, a human. A first for him in his eternal life.

"I need to know something. Can you accept that there are things in this world beyond the human? That when people do horrible things to each other, and you think to yourself that they're evil, they really are? And that when someone should have died and didn't, through some miracle, that there really were angels at work? Can you accept these ideas as truth, Callie?" He stared steadily into her eyes, and for a few moments, he wondered if she'd ever respond.

She gave him a cold, hard glare. "My parents were brutally murdered by vicious, sadistic men. I was raped repeatedly by a psycho for a fake brother. Oh yes, yes, I believe people are evil. But that's where it ends." She tore her hands away from his and flitted them in the air. "Where were these supposed angels of yours to save my father, my mother, to save me? Hmmm?"

He stood and slunk over to the dresser, turning to lean on it for support. "They do exist."

"Oh, really?" She scoffed. "And how do you know this?"

He took a deep breath. "I'm one of them."

Silence and a look of incredulity smacked him in the face.

"Oh, my God! You're a total whack job!" She sprang up and thrust her hand out. "Just give me the envelope and leave. Right now!"

"Callie, I'm an angel and immortal. So is the entire Brethren Security team." He pulled the edge of his T-shirt over his head. She had to see his wings or she wouldn't trust him.

"What the hell do you think you're doing? Put your shirt back on!" She'd skirted over to the desk and grabbed the lamp like a baseball bat.

"Easy. I want to show you my wings." He thought about them for a fraction of a second and with the grace of a butterfly, they unfurled from shoulder to ankle.

First, she dropped the lamp, and then she dropped herself.

"Shit," he muttered as he crossed the floor to her crumpled body. He scooped her up, laid her on the bed, and fanned her face with a hotel room service menu while sitting on the edge, waiting for her to come to. Being a Warrior, not a Savior, there wasn't a whole lot more he could do. She'd awaken when she awakened.

He watched intently until her eyes fluttered open and rested upon him...and his wings. He shifted uneasily where he sat. Her eyes widened and her jaw dropped as the seconds passed. She shoved her body to an upright position, never taking her eyes off of him.

"Aren't you going to say anything?"

"You...you're an angel."

"Yup." He sure wished he knew what she planned to do about it.

"Kemuel?" She ran shaky fingers through her hair.

"He's one, too. And so is Raphael."

"Huh." She shook her head and a slight pink flush crept up her neck to her cheeks. "I...I can't deny what I'm seeing right in front of me. But at the same time I can't believe it. This is the last thing I expected you to say or show me. Where do I begin to understand your existence? How many of you are there?"

"Nine at the moment. Two Warriors, like me, three Saviors, and three Protectors. And there's Emma, who's our Great Savior Mother."

"Huh. I bet Kemuel is probably a Warrior, right? Raphael, a Savior? Oh, my God! Does Serena know?"

"Yes, on all counts, and Serena is actually immortal as well."

"Dear Lord," she murmured, and covered her face with her hands.

He moved toward her and placed a tentative hand on hers. "Are you okay?"

She shoved it off and looked at him with angry eyes laden with resentment.

Here it comes. Hold steady, man.

Years of hurt, anger, and bitterness engulfed Callie, and welled up like a dormant volcano come back to life. With a wail rivaling the banshees of folklore, she leapt from the bed and let loose with a sharp smack across his face.

Hard.

Her hand vibrated with the pain and sting of it.

"Where were all of you? Why didn't you save my parents? Why didn't you save me? My life is so screwed up! I hate you! You hear me?" With each word she pounded upon his chest, nailing into him all the anguish and rage she'd suppressed over the years. "I hate you! I hate you! I hate you!" Tears streamed down her cheeks in a torrent as sobs poured from her mouth.

He hugged her to him, restricting her arms and hands. "I'm so sorry, Callie. We didn't know. We didn't know. Shh...." He kissed her head and rubbed her back. She struggled to free herself, but with no energy left, her legs gave way.

The pair crumpled to the bed and as he rocked her, she cried in a small, childlike voice, "I hate you. I hate you. I hate you...."

"I'm so sorry. I'm here for you now, though. I'm right here and I'm not going anywhere. We'll fix things now." She whimpered as his fingers slid through her hair and massaged her scalp. "Let me fix things. Let me fix you."

His words were a soothing tonic, a hypnotizing mantra in her head that she didn't want to stop. She sniffled and hiccupped. One minute blended into another as she held on to him, the only lifeline in a world spinning out of control.

"I don't really hate you." She spoke softly after minutes of silence. "I...couldn't...." She hiccupped again. "Hate you. You're too freakin' nice." She shook her head gently and looked up into his beautiful green eyes, seeking unspoken forgiveness for her abrasive words. She rubbed her lips together and moistened them with her tongue.

Nathanael cupped her cheek and caressed it with the pad of his thumb. He leaned in slowly until he was but a hair's breadth away from her face, and then closed the distance to kiss her oh-so-gently. She lost herself in the warmth and pressure of his lips, and tears started anew as her heart skipped a beat from the simplicity of it all. As they parted, he looked bewildered. Her own shock met his. But she couldn't help herself. She needed him desperately, man and angel. She needed to replace her scarred memories with something as beautiful and wondrous as an angel's kiss. So she touched her hands to his face and guided him back to her lips.

She whispered against him, "I need you, Nathanael." Her mouth laid siege upon his, and he retaliated with all the fervor of a man who'd been swept away. He pulled her impossibly closer as she slid her hands up his well-defined chest and wrapped her arms around his neck.

She was tired of the hurt, through with being scared, and knew, with him, having sex would be very different. It would be making love. Something she personally didn't know a thing about. The capacity to hope for something as pure as that had been stolen from her a very long time ago. It had been replaced with a driving need to prove she was alive and could feel and have all the control. And that, she decided while kissing the brains out of an angel, was exactly what she would rely on right now.

He released her lips to make a trail of kisses around her jaw line to right behind her ear. And shivering, she let him. She let him kiss the sweet spot where her neck and shoulder met. She let him caress her breasts with the gentlest of touches. And she let him stop.

Breathing heavily, he dropped his hands and looked at her with apologetic eyes. "I'm sorry. I didn't mean to...I...well, yes. Yes, I did mean to. But this is no time to be distracted by temptation. And it certainly isn't the right time or place for how I'd like it to be for you, with you."

She chuckled, straightened her shirt, and sighed ruefully. "You really are an angel, ain'tcha? It's a shame." She tapped him on the cheek and smiled. "Well, I guess we all have some crazy shit about us." She rose and padded over to the window to peer out at the bright lights. *Figures he'd pull the gentleman card.*

"Wow. Not quite the reaction I thought I'd receive. I mean, you fainted, you got angry. I expected that. But now, you're acting as though who I am is nothing unusual."

"I only fainted because you took me by surprise." She paused, not ready to give up her tough-girl persona quite yet. "What more do you want from me? A couple of intense kisses, as much as I wanted and needed them, doesn't change who I am. I'm still a fucked-up, hard-assed woman in a lot of danger, and you...you're still Nate, the bounty hunter. Only with wings."

"Don't you have any questions for me?" He approached her. She noticed he took a deep breath, and his wings receded. He put his shirt on and tucked it back in his pants.

"I already know you can beat the shit out of anyone, and that you probably can't get hurt. So, as a bodyguard, you pretty well rock." She turned to face him. "Oh wait, I do have one question. How do you keep those things so white?"

"You know, you're really something."

"I told you. Now if you'll excuse me, my little breakdown did nothing for my makeup." She pushed past him, picked up her bag, and went to the bathroom.

"Well, when you get out, I need to share something else with you."

"Sure, sure," she called out from behind the door. She leaned against it and took in a deep breath, letting it out slowly. *Oh, my God! He's a true-blue angel! And so are my friends! What on earth do I do with that? I don't have a freakin' clue. One thing I do know, Serena and I are having a long chat when this mess is all over. I wonder, though. Maybe I should tell him about the Elixxir now.*

Chapter Nine

Holy shit! For having revealed himself to a human woman for the first time in his immortal life, it went pretty strangely. He'd never asked Michael or Raphael how it had gone for them when they'd shared who they were to Emma and Serena. He'd flown by the seat of his pants, and prayed he hadn't made the worst mistake in his eternal life. Traversing the jungles of Vietnam seemed easier than dealing with this woman he'd just shackled himself to. He rubbed the back of his neck, trying to predict who'd be walking out of the bathroom in a few minutes—sweet-and-vulnerable Callie or snarky Callie.

Either way, she tested him like no other. And he liked it. When he'd kissed her earlier, he'd gotten a glimpse into her psyche and found she'd played him through every part of their romantic exchange. Had he been human, he would have thought he'd been the dominant one throughout the entire situation. But his warrior senses allowed him unprecedented access to the minds of the people he connected with, and hers was undeniably secured by threads of control he would take pleasure in slowly unwinding. She needed to know there were some men in this world that weren't looking to victimize her. He would undoubtedly be her first.

Now that she knew about him, he also decided he would tell her his true mission: to secure the Elixxir of Life back to the

Beyond. Maybe, if she knew the implications of it falling into the wrong hands, she'd be more willing to open up and share whatever information she had. The way he figured, she already knew she didn't want the bad guys to get it, but she had no clue that the Elixxir was real. Her motivations ran along the lines that it belonged to her parents and now her, and it could be stolen away forever.

Callie opened the bathroom door feeling more determined than ever. "Okay, Nate, let's open up Pandora's Box. It's now or never."

"Here, you open it. It's only right." He handed the envelope to her and she sat on the unfamiliar bed, wishing it were her own. Crossing her legs, she tried to get comfortable.

She slid a finger under the glued flap, stuffed her hand inside, and pulled out a paper. "Jesus Christ. It's a letter. From my father. It's dated. Lord, this letter's twenty years old." Taking a calming breath, she began reading aloud.

"Dearest Ariana, if you are reading this letter, then my first attempt to conceal the Elixxir has failed and something terrible has happened to your mother and me. But I have two more safeguards and pray they work. I am so sorry to have put you in this horrible position. I didn't think at the time it could get this bad. The Elixxir's appeal has grown since I've acquired it, and it has become too dangerous to keep. I never thought people would actually believe in its powers like I do, but they do and have become crazed with hunger for its gift. For this reason, I've hidden it rather than put it on display in the shop. You won't be able to see it now, but right below this letter, I've written directions to where it can be found. I hope you remember how we used to write notes to each other. When you find the Elixxir, get rid of it! It will surely cause you nothing but more pain. And then hide. Evil people are circling and will not rest until they get their hands on it and kill everyone connected to it. Your life, I'm afraid, has forever been altered by my foolish greed. Instead of living forever, I am probably damned to Hell. I am so sorry, my dearest child. So very sorry. Dad."

She sat stone still for a few minutes, rolling his message over and over in her mind.

"Are you okay?"

"Yeah, yeah, I'm fine. And now you know what someone's willing to blow up an apartment and kill for."

He nodded. "The Elixxir of Life."

"Yes, do you know anything about it?"

"It is known to bring immortality to anyone who drinks it."

"It's a bunch of bullshit, if you ask me. It's probably a flask filled with tap water."

"It's true. The Elixxir is real, and if it falls into the wrong hands it will be disastrous on so many levels. Evil will grow rampant and overtake the Good."

She scoffed. "Come on, Nate. My father's shop had some cool knick-knacks and oddities in it, but something as far-fetched as this is...is...just that! Far-fetched! A bunch of hooey."

"I'm on a mission to retrieve this hooey and bring it back into secure hands."

"What? Are you serious?"

"Totally."

"This whole situation gets more outrageous the longer I'm in it. Wait a minute. You came to my apartment looking for it, didn't you? Your visit had nothing to do with Kemuel's apology at all, did it?"

"Yes, he really asked me to apologize for him. And yes, I'd already been assigned my mission to find the Elixxir when I came knocking at your door."

Overwhelmed by his disclosure, she ran out of the room.

She ran down hall after hall until she knew what the hell she wanted to do next. Next turned out to be finding a stairwell and sitting on a step to clear her muddled head.

He could have caught up with her easily. But he chose to let her go. Her world had spun out of her control, and if running and hiding for a while would bring things back into balance for her, he would give that to her. He laughed at her attempt to get away from him as he sauntered down the hallway. She'd stopped in Stairwell B, Floor 19. Warrior tracking senses came in so handy for many purposes, not only for hunting criminals. They were great for keeping a distant eye on the people he cared about. And he cared about her. Keeping her safe wasn't strictly business. It had become a personal mission, as well. He couldn't deny that. But securing the Elixxir had to be top priority for the safety of the world.

He lightly pushed open the door to the stairwell. Rather than simply floating down to her, he decided instead to walk each step, giving her a little time and space. He found her sitting on one, leaning against the wall between the twentieth and nineteenth floors.

Nathanael lowered himself onto the one above her and stretched his legs. She didn't so much as even flinch. "Hey." He rubbed her back and kneaded the knots of tension bunched beneath his fingers.

"Hey."

"I know this is a lot to take in. It's not every day you learn that angels exist and that by drinking a liquid you can become immortal. I get it. I'm hoping we can move forward, though. That Elixxir must be found and secured as soon as possible. Can I count on you to help me?"

She turned around and raised a brow. "Oh, now you're *asking* me for help? Tell me, you've known, since I found you at my doorstep, that I had the Elixxir."

"Yes, I can't lie. So yes, I did know. And what about you? You knew all along the men were after the Elixxir, didn't you?"

"Yes."

He got up, moved down a couple of stairs, and turned so they were face to face. He leaned against a raised knee. "Then you are no different than me. We are both secretive and have very good reasons to be so. I am protecting the world, and you, well, you are protecting the remnants of a life so radically changed from what it should have been."

"No, I guess in that sense we're not that different. So, when we find this Elixxir, what do you plan on doing with it?"

"I have to take it back to the Beyond where it will be secured for eternity."

"And what if I don't want to give it to you? What if I want to keep it? What would you do?"

"I would have to find a way to convince you to give it to me. It can't remain here. It's not meant for this world."

"I don't want it anyway," she said dismissively. "It's caused me nothing but suffering and pain." She nudged him out of the way and walked up the steps at an unhurried pace. "We need to go to a novelty shop and get an invisible ink kit. I know it sounds silly, but that's what I'm sure my father used to write the rest of the letter. That's what he was telling me when he wrote about us writing notes to each other. We always used invisible ink."

"That should be easy enough to find."

"My father's store had them in a section for kids. What do you say we tempt the fates and go there?"

He charged up the stairs and grabbed her by the arm to stop and turn her toward him. "I don't know if you're a bold, kickass woman or just one with a death wish."

"I've been wondering what Uncle's done with the place. And who knows, if we decipher the letter, it might lead us back there."

"There's not a chance I'm letting you go there yet. Not until we know who's a part of this death plot. We can find something at one of the shops around here."

She shrugged. "It was worth a shot. You know, if I remember my father well, and I think I do, he's not going to make this easy for us. He loved puzzles, and if he thought danger surrounded this thing, he could have cloaked its whereabouts in a riddle or something like that."

"Well, we'll see soon enough. Come on." He held out his hand to her. "This is one clue the bad guys don't have. Hopefully, the note they took doesn't tell them everything."

She nodded and put her hand in his as he turned to walk

back up the steps.

"Nathanael."

"Yes?"

"Stop a minute." He did as she bade him, and waited for her to reach a few steps above him.

"All my secrets are revealed. My cards played. How about yours?"

Her gaze sought an assurance he couldn't give her. She would have to understand there were things he could never share with her. "As far as the Elixxir goes, I have told you everything I know and what I need to do. Beyond that, I can't promise to tell you everything about me, about the Brethren, about the world beyond. It is too much of a risk. But you must know that what I do share with you, I've never shared with another human. I am trusting you with our existence and the safety of its secrecy. Think you can handle that?"

"You can trust me. I'll never tell."

He smiled and they continued back to their room. *Raphael can always do a mind sweep if you do.*

☙

Las Vegas, Nevada

Classical music lilting in the background did nothing to soothe his irritation. Ariana still lived. His men would arrive shortly with the envelope they'd found in the wreckage of her apartment. He suspected it contained information about the Elixxir flask. Ruminating about the plan he'd conceived years ago, he grinned for the first time that day. She would be brought to him, alive. Then, she would be forced to watch as he drank the Elixxir. Finally, she would die and he would live. Forever. At least that was the plan for now. Things could always change.

"Mr. Murati, there are two gentlemen waiting in the foyer to see you."

"Send them in, Clara. Thank you." He swirled the brandy in

the snifter and took a swill. *Ah, sweet.* But revenge would be sweeter. He relaxed into his wing-back chair by the stone fireplace.

Two well-dressed men entered the library and stood before him. "Please, gentlemen, take a seat. You have something for me, Johnny?"

The man with the shiny, charcoal gray Armani suit answered. "Yes, sir. As I told you over the phone, we found the envelope in a safe. There's a return address on it for a law office here in Vegas. It's sealed. Looks like it's never been opened. Here." He handed it to him.

"Good, good. Nice work, you two. Stay here while I open it. I may have another assignment for you."

He took the letter opener that rested on a side table and sliced through the flap, imagining it to be Ariana's neck. He took out the note and painstakingly unfolded it. "Son of a bitch!" He tossed it to the floor.

"What is it, Mr. Murati?" Marco spoke up this time.

"It's a damn puzzle! A friggin' clue! Even from the grave Joseph toys with me! I don't have time to play his stupid games." He swallowed the rest of the brandy in one swig.

"So now what, boss?"

"Isn't it obvious? As much as I loathe what he's done to me, we must solve the puzzle and go from there. Johnny!" He held out his glass. "Pour me another brandy. Marco, pick up the damn letter and let's get started figuring out the answer."

Chapter Ten

Callie found a novelty shop not far from their hotel. Although within walking distance, given the fact it neared midnight, taking the bike seemed a safer bet. It made for easy getaways, if necessary. As they pulled up to the storefront, she had second thoughts. It looked like a tiny hole in the wall. But as she dismounted, she mustered up her optimism and put a smile on her face. It didn't matter what the place looked like, really. Having called beforehand, she knew they had what they were looking for.

As she opened the door, the ear-piercing jingle of a bell alerted the world they had arrived. The young girl at the counter near the front of the store immediately looked up from her book and blew a bubble with her gum.

"Hi, we're having a sale on crystal balls today. Forty percent off. And if you're interested in fake vomit, it's buy one, get one free." She went back to reading and chewing like a cow.

"Thank you." Nathanael sidled up next to Callie, leaned on the counter, and smiled a toothy grin. "We were actually interested in your invisible ink kits. We have a nephew who's into all that spy stuff. Can you help us find one?"

And help we're gonna need, Callie thought to herself as she looked around. The minuscule store had only two aisles and floor-to-ceiling shelves crammed with all sorts of magic and comic paraphernalia. It suffocated.

The girl gave him a sour smile in return. "Invisible ink kits are down aisle two, all the way at the end, right side, second shelf from the bottom."

Following the clerk's directions, Callie eyed what she needed and turned to say so, but when she did, she found him still standing by the counter, watching her. After giving him a quizzical look, she finally understood. He motioned with his hands that the width of the aisle was narrower than the width of him. She laughed, picked up the kit, and headed back toward the front. He paid, and they headed back to the hotel, stopping only to pick up a pizza and drinks.

ᙂ

"I'm so glad we stopped for something to eat. My stomach growled something fierce the whole time we were in the store."

"I know. I heard it." Nathanael put his hands against his ears, and she smacked his arm with the back of her hand. They shared a mushroom pepperoni pie, picnic-style, on the bed.

"You know something? I think pizza tastes better the later the evening gets, don't you?"

"I can eat the damn stuff morning, noon, and night. Don't know why, and I don't question it." He smiled back. "Do you want to do the reveal now? I can tell you're utterly exhausted at this point."

"I am, but I want to know what my father wrote. So, let me at it. Where'd you put the kit?"

"On the table. Where's the letter?"

"In my bag." She grabbed it and sat down across from him.

He read the directions on the back of the package. "Hmm, says here we're supposed to spray this liquid on the paper and the chemical reacts with the ink. Here." He took the small spray bottle out of the plastic cover and handed it to her. Would the ink still react after all this time? Nate looked dubious, but she disregarded his cynicism and hoped for the best.

"Thanks. Here goes everything."

She spritzed the paper with a fine coating and waited. Not ten seconds later, a message appeared. She sprang from her seat. "Here it is! Nate, it worked!" She calmed herself and sat back down. "Listen to this. *With a find such as this, I'd be foolish to disclose its whereabouts plainly. There are clues to be found and rules to be followed. Here's your first clue: Where the lions sleep and roar is a marquee with a trap door. A quarter past noon is the best time for you to open it and solve Clue #2.*"

"You weren't kidding when you said he liked puzzles, were ya?"

"Nope. God, reading his words, I…. It's like I can almost hear his voice again." She shook herself from her reverie. "Well, I know exactly where we need to go. It's a place we used to go all the time as a family. The Big Cats Safari Refuge. It has a lion habitat in it. We have to find the right marquee and wait until a quarter past noon to retrieve the next clue!"

"Respectfully, I must say that as much as your father meant for this to be a game, it's not. Your life is in danger. I'm sure with my skills I can get the next clue regardless of time and without a problem."

"Okay, well I'm really bushwhacked and my brain could use a break for a couple hours. I'm gonna turn in for a bit. You must be tired as well."

"Angels never sleep."

"What? That's crazy! How do you keep your energy up?"

"We meditate for a bit every now and then, but that's all we need." He picked up a napkin and gently wiped the corner of her mouth. "You had some sauce on ya, sorry. Didn't want you to be embarrassed later."

"Thanks." Callie brushed her hands off over the empty box and closed it. They'd polished the whole thing off in about fifteen minutes. "So what are you going to do while I sleep?"

"I'm gonna go work out. I've been carrying a lot of pent-up energy since the bus station incident and need to get rid of it."

"Pent-up energy, huh?" She smothered a giggle.

"Yeah, I need to pound on something hard and long, or I'm gonna burst."

"Nathanael, sweetheart, let me clue you in." She shook her head. "You don't go telling a girl something like that and then leave for the gym."

"I don't know what the hell you are talking about." He got up from the bed and headed toward the door.

"Think about it as you're heading downstairs, okay?"

"Whatever. Don't answer the door or the phone for any reason. I'll be back in about a half hour."

"Okay. Have fun sweating it up, alone."

He knew exactly what Callie had alluded to upstairs, but the energy he'd kept a lid on all day and night could not be controlled once let out. He'd hurt her. So he chose to call his friend to box him to a pulp instead. At least he would be able to recover from it, like any immortal. Joe showed up at the world-class fitness room, as requested, and Nathanael proceeded to pummel the immortal crap out of him. Joe returned the favor.

"Wow, you're definitely wound up tighter than a jack-in-the-box. What's up?" They sat on the floor, sweat pouring down their faces, guzzling water from their bottles.

"Had a little run-in with some jerk-offs at the bus station earlier. Laid them all out flat in like five seconds. Got my mojo going strong and had nowhere to put it. Nearly knocked Callie flat on her ass."

"What? That's no good, man."

"I didn't, Joe. She said my name, and I stopped. She pulled me out of my crazies."

"You used to be able to do it yourself."

"I know, I know." He took a long draw on his water bottle.

"Dude, you don't want to go there." He put a hand on Nathanael's shoulder. "Trust me. I didn't turn from my demon ways because I'm a pussy. Nothing good can happen if you follow that path. It's pure Evil, through and through."

"I don't know what to do, Joe!" He threw his bottle across

the room. "I can't just stop. I have a job to do. Not only the bounty hunting, but Brethren business. I'm a freakin' Warrior and I kill evil people. The rush fills me. It charges me up. It gives me something I can't get from anything else."

"But you're not in control anymore. It's controlling you. That's serious. That sounds like addiction to me."

"Are you saying I'm a violence addict?" He shot up and started pacing back and forth.

"I'm saying you're addicted to the rush of adrenaline you get every time you battle. And it's getting worse. You gotta do something about it."

"Like what? Go all peace activist?" He snorted. "That's not realistic."

"No, but you can cut down on the amount of scuffles and battles you engage in."

Nathanael stopped abruptly and kneeled down in front of Joe. In a hushed voice he spoke. "He gets to me. When it's over, Satan gets right to my heart and my head and toys with me. Teases me with promises of infinite power and glory, and an end to my guilt complex over my abilities. And I want to succumb. How the hell do I break away from that?"

"You need to stay away from violence. And you need a sponsor. I can be that for you. Think about it and get back to me. But don't wait too long or something dreadful is bound to happen. Now, I gotta go. Time to scour the streets to save some possessed souls. Call me, bro. Sooner than later."

"Yeah, yeah...."

Working out should have done him well, but instead, after talking with Joe, he bristled like a caged lion all over again. Two by two, he took the stairs all the way up twenty-two flights. When he reached the door to his room, he slid the key in the lock and quietly opened the door. A shower was definitely called for at this point, so he entered the bathroom, stripped, and started the water running. When the steam enveloped the room, he stepped into the hot rain falling from the ceiling, closed his eyes, and wondered how long he'd been fooling himself. Every time he killed in the name of Brethren justice, Satan sneaked into his subconscious and tested his resolve, filling him with the sense of infinite power. And he reveled in it! But like a drug, the euphoria lingered only so long, and each time, it lessened in duration.

Frustration overwhelmed him and he banged a fist against the shower wall, letting the steady stream pummel his already pounding head. Why had E.L. refused to help him? Hadn't asking him what he should do months ago been enough proof that he wanted to stay Brethren? Did he have to test his resolve now as well?

Suddenly, out of the corner of his eye, he saw the shower curtain undulate and heard the door click. Damn, he hadn't heard it open!

"Nate? Are you okay?" Callie's voice slid seductively in between the pelting water music.

He wasn't.

And he couldn't lie. He wouldn't. Not to her.

"No, I'm not."

She moved the curtain aside, but he refused to turn around, choosing to remain leaning against the back wall. He sensed her step in behind him and rest a gentle hand on his back.

"What are you doing?" His voice shook with restraint.

"I'm here to see what's wrong. Nathanael, tell me what's wrong."

The insistent tone broke through his crumbling defenses. He reached behind him, grasped her hands, and pulled her close to wrap her body around his like a safety shroud. He held on, as though he would fall into an abyss otherwise.

"Jesus!" As she spoke, she clutched him even tighter. "What can I do? Just tell me. What?"

"Tell me I'm good."

He waited. The crashing of water against his shoulders filled the space meant to reassure him of his worth. Even should she reply so, would he believe? Satan had been messing with him for so long now, he didn't believe in much of anything anymore.

"Holy shit, Nate. You are! You're all that is good and right in this world."

"No, no I'm not. You don't know me. I don't know me. Not anymore."

Callie pulled away from his grip and turned his body around to face her. She swiped his hair away from his face and caressed his cheeks. "What's gotten into you?" Her gaze sought understanding from him, but he had nothing comforting to give.

"Evil! Evil's gotten into me, and I don't know how to get it out! Or even if I want to let it go!"

She stood silent and staring, her soaked T-shirt and boxers like a second skin, her matted hair streaming in wet bands of brilliant red, an oasis for his eyes. And then the unexpected came. She slapped him so hard across his face it stung.

"Snap out of it! You're a freakin' Brethren Warrior, for Christ's sake! Kick it the hell out of ya!"

He rubbed his cheek, surprised by her tactics. "It's not that simple. I could have hurt you today." He rested his arms on her shoulders and clasped his hands behind her head. She lowered hers and then looked up at him with a sage's eyes.

"Nothing ever is easy, is it? We just gotta fight the good fight every day. And you didn't hurt me. You stopped."

"But I could next time. I need help. I've needed help for a while. I'm an addict."

"You do drugs?" Her eyes widened.

"No, I do violence. I fight and kill in the name of Brethren justice and get high on the rush. It's gotten to the point where the high hasn't been lasting as long as it used to, and I seek out more and more situations and people I can feed off of."

"Do the other Warriors react the same way? Have you talked about this with them?"

"No, I haven't, but I don't see them behave the way I do after we battle. I tell you, Satan's gotten to me. He wants me, and I don't know how much longer I can fight him."

"Let's call his bluff, then. Find something that gives you the same thrill, the same rush, and one that is more acceptable for you."

"I don't have the first clue what that could be."

"I do." She slid her hands around his waist until they met, and rose up on her tiptoes. "Come here." Her eyes fluttered closed, and he knew exactly what she wanted.

Mesmerized, he obeyed. He leaned down and captured her lips with his. They were welcoming and a gateway to promised peace. His hands had minds of their own, and each found a sweet spot, one cradling her head, and the other caressing her back, bringing her closer so their bodies were as one. She deepened the kiss and, feeling the coolness of her drenched clothes, he brought her under the cascading warmth of the shower. Releasing his mouth, she focused on kissing the edges of his lips and jaw line. A hopeful thought caused him to smile.

Callie opened her eyes and frowned. "Do my kisses amuse you that much?"

He laughed and kissed her hard. "Not at all," he said heatedly. "In fact, I think Satan may have met his match with you."

"You won't know, now will you, until you put my theory to the test."

Without further delay, he pulled the hem of her T-shirt over her head and tossed the sopping mess on the floor of the shower. She stepped out of her boxers and opened her arms to him.

"Come to me."

A goddess stood before him, he could have sworn, with rivulets of water making paths down her body that he longed to re-trace with his tongue. He took a step toward her.

"You're so beautiful, Callie."

"Ariana. Can you call me Ariana, please?" she asked quietly, and peered up at him with a combination of innocence and fortitude. In return, he put his immortal life in her hands. Hope bloomed where just a short time ago, darkness filled his soul. Astounded by her strength and courage, he dared to believe, at least for now, that he might be able to keep his angel soul from flaming out and falling irrevocably into the depths of Hell.

"Save me, Ariana."

Nathanael gathered her in his arms, feasting on her lips as though they were a succulent treat. She found, awakening within her, the woman she thought had long since died by a kiss so diametrically opposed to this one. A healthy, untarnished sensuality blossomed. She feared it as much as she embraced it. Her heart thrummed as his need pressed against her belly and his kisses blazed a trail down her neck.

He stepped back from her, knelt down, and pressed feather-light kisses along her ribcage. One hand cupped her breast, massaging and teasing her into an involuntary moan. His tongue traced the path of one water droplet inching its way down her body. And he took his own sweet time as well, nipping and lapping along the way, creating little explosions of pleasure, until he arrived at her core. And there he lingered.

"I'll save you," she murmured deliriously. "I'll save you. Oh, God." His tender touch created goose bumps, and frissons of excitement skittered across her skin.

He worked his way back up again and swept her off her feet. Moving the curtains aside, he stepped out of the tub. "Open the door for me, would you?" he asked, his voice husky and deep.

She fumbled with the knob, but finally pulled it as he took a step back. His chest expanded as he breathed in deeply, and suddenly, she saw his wings peek out over his shoulders and unfurl. Breathless with anticipation, waves of ecstasy threatened to drown her. The thought of making love with an angel compounded the thrill.

The bed seemed a million miles away, but in the blink of an eye, they were hovering together, bodies entwined, just beside it. She watched as a wave of doubt washed over his face. Emboldened, Ariana spoke. "Don't be shy with me now. You won't hurt me. Let me show you how good you really are."

Mesmerized by his wings' iridescence, she moved to touch them. As she did so, individual feathers fluttered, his grip tightened around her waist, and he moaned. She combed her fingers through the outer feathers and he shivered in her arms.

She continued to stroke his wings, and while watching his control fade away minute by minute, hers did as well. Little bolts of energy fired throughout her body, sending heated impulses straight to her womb.

"Lord, I need you inside me. Take me now!" Holding on to his shoulders, she jumped up and locked her legs around his waist.

"Oh, God! Yes!" His feverish eyes spoke of his need as he eased her down onto him.

"Oh!" She gasped, overwhelmed by the fullness and completeness of him buried inside her.

They rocked in unison, as though they'd been created for each other. His heart pounded against her breasts in a synchronized rhythm to hers. As he moved them over to the bed, they consumed each other with kisses and breathed as one. Never before had sex been like this to her. In her passionate haze, a thought entered her mind. *This isn't merely sex. This is making love.*

Faster and harder she pumped while straddling him until she crested the peak of rapture. He cried out her name, and his whole body trembled beneath her, even his wings. And then he stilled. She fell upon his chest, panting and smiling, amazed, and totally sated. His arms came around her, shifting her to his side, and held her tenderly as his wings enclosed them in a protective cocoon. Lulled by the soothing touch of feathers against her skin, she fell asleep.

Chapter Eleven

𝒜 distinctive aroma invaded Ariana's swirling dreams, rousing her and teasing her to wake up and smell the coffee. Without opening her eyes, she reached up and grasped a hand holding a mug she knew was right under her nose. Sipping at the rim, she groaned her sweet pleasure and raised the curtains of her eyelids. Nathanael, crouched by her bedside, shook his head and laughed.

"Hey, you have your addiction. I have mine. Now release the mug, man." She squirmed up to a semi-sitting position and raised her brow, waiting for him to relinquish his hold.

"I don't know how you can like this stuff, but I figured you were probably a coffee kinda girl." He let go and sat next to her on the bed.

"It's the nectar of the gods. How can you, of all people, not like it?"

"I like beer. That's my nectar." He shrugged. "Spending centuries on the frontlines and covertly in black ops, I got accustomed to relaxing when I could with a beer. I don't need caffeine to keep me awake, so it's a waste."

"Good point, I guess. So you're military through and through, huh?"

"Yup, and this military man says it's time to get up and uncover your father's mysterious message. But first, about last night, Callie—Ariana.... Hey, what do you want me to call you?"

"I'm done with hiding behind a name. Call me by who I really am: Ariana. And Nate, your secret is safe with me. I'll do whatever it takes to keep you on the up side of this world. Okay?"

"Okay." He cleared his throat. "I sure wouldn't mind you doing whatever it takes if it's anything like last night."

She rolled her eyes and punched him in the arm. "It's a hard job, but someone has to do it." With her coffee in one hand, she managed to get out of bed without spilling it everywhere and headed for the bathroom. "Give me ten minutes and I'll be ready." In case he had any notion of following her, she locked the door.

Nathanael's cell phone vibrated in his pants pocket. He had a text message. Gabriel. The new member of the Brethren had been chosen and he'd manifested earlier this morning. Gabriel had orders to bring the newbie to him for training. *Great. Not what I needed right now. A newbie underfoot.* His phone buzzed again. *Ah, his name is Yofi.* He texted Gabriel his location. *Then again, maybe another Brethren brain isn't such a bad idea. He may be able to help us find the Elixxir that much sooner.*

Ɔɘ

Murati's Curiosity Shop
Las Vegas

Eddie sat confidently in his chair in the back office. He hadn't felt this great in years. Twenty, to be exact. He was a new man with a new agenda, and a new lease on life. *Screw the Marchese drug cartel and the rest of them douchebags, for that matter!* He would take each one of them down and have a monopoly without the fear of being killed in the process. He strode over to the wall safe and dialed the requisite numbers until a click told him it had unlocked. He carefully opened the door and took out a small, plain brass box. The patina spoke of centuries of weathering, beautiful all on its own. But the treasure it held inside spoke volumes more. He lifted the lid gingerly and gazed upon the most prized possession in the world. The Elixxir of Life.

A hard knock jolted him from his euphoria. He'd locked the door earlier so no one could disturb him, and chosen to keep it that way.

"Yes!" he barked. "What is it?"

"Mr. Murati," Johnny's deep timbre easily identified him. "The real clues have been destroyed and replaced with fakes just like you said to. I made sure they'll send whoever finds them on a wild goose chase."

"Excellent! You've done well, for a change. Go home."

"Thank you, sir."

Whoever sought out the Elixxir, and there were many greedy bastards out there like him still clamoring for it, would never find it now. It would remain secure with him forever. He closed the box's lid and returned it to the safe, sensing youthfulness and vibrancy thrum through every cell and atom in his body. Finding the flask, using only the crumbs of clues Joseph had left behind, enraged him, but in the end, he had the last laugh—and a sip. He thought he could wait for Ariana to watch the ultimate insult, and he'd been so good for a while, but it proved to be too enticing and he'd taken a long swig of the bitter liquid a few hours ago.

Immortality is mine!

Now, to tie up all the loose ends and find the bitch! And find her, he would. He blamed her for twenty years of fruitless searching for the damned thing. Dear old Watkins, the family lawyer, had been a surprising disappointment. Even to his dying breath, he wouldn't divulge its whereabouts. Only that it remained safely with her.

He'd spent those twenty years paying off anyone and everyone who could give him the slightest clue where to find her.

But the irony of it all? She'd put the nail in her own coffin! Just a few days ago she'd somehow revealed her whereabouts online. With her and anyone else who threatened his new existence out of the way, he saw his endgame clearly in sight.

World domination.

He looked at his reflection in the shiny blackness of the safe and grinned. Orbs of glowing red replaced his typical muddy brown eyes. His grin grew into a chuckle. And the chuckle erupted into a cackle of the most wicked kind.

ᜒ

"Well, now we know why my father gave us a specific time to come here," Ariana complained as they stood off to the side of the entrance watching hordes of visitors walk under the Lion Habitat sign without a break in sight. "All these folks probably go eat at the *Dine With the Cats* lunch and show at that time. What are we gonna do?"

"No worries. I got it all under control."

"Oh, really? And how do you think we're gonna find that one loose wooden plank and get the clue while everyone is treading all over it?"

"Leave it to me. I'm an angel, remember? I have shields so no one can see me or detect me if I don't want them to. An added benefit is that anything I touch is shielded as well."

"Shields, huh?" She didn't sound very impressed. "Okay, fine. Do your angel thing. I'll just wait over here by the directory."

She continued to surprise him with her nonchalant attitude. But then again, it made things a whole lot easier for him. He watched her plant herself on the ground to sit and wait by a huge sign telling folks where they were in the park. When traffic by the entrance slowed down enough, he shielded, made his way over to the area, and tapped each board under the marquee with his foot to find a loose one.

Under the L of "Lion Habitat", he found it. Squatting, he

touched all around the edges for some kind of handhold. There were none, so he opted for pounding a fist soundly on one side and up popped the other. He grabbed the plank, now at a peculiar angle to the ground, and held it steady with one hand as he dipped the other into the hole it had created. A few grasps at air and then he hit paydirt, a small metal box. He thrust it into his back pocket, replaced the wooden plank, and returned to Ariana.

He whispered in her ear, "Red, I'm right next to you. Only you can hear me. Walk to the casino exit. I'll be right next to you the whole time. When we reach an alcove, duck in and I'll unshield."

"Gotta admit that's the coolest thing I've ever seen, Nate. Or not seen, I guess. Do you have the clue?"

"I retrieved a small box. Don't know if it's the clue yet. Let's move."

She jumped up and started walking toward the exit. An alcove led to restrooms and telephones, so she turned in. After a few people strolled by, the area cleared, and he dropped his shields. He opened the box and a small, folded piece of paper rested inside.

"Let me scan this thing out before we read it, okay?"

"Sure, do what you gotta do."

He unfolded the paper and closed his eyes, hoping the threads on this paper hadn't degraded as badly as on the first one. Any residual threads of intent and motivation, anything that remained on the person's mind when they wrote and handled the paper, would be sensed and understood by him. If he could, he would know immediately where the Elixxir lay stowed, saving them inordinate amounts of time searching for clue upon clue. He put a flat palm on its surface and rubbed.

"Shit and double shit," he growled.

Ariana immediately grabbed the paper from his hands. "Let me see it." She looked down and read the note. "What's the problem? I know exactly where we need to go next."

"It's a fake. Meant to throw us off or lead us into a trap. Someone's gotten to the clues and replaced them with their own. Damn it."

"How the hell do you know that?"

"Can I have it back, please?" He held out his hand. "You took it from me before I could finish tracking the threads."

She offered it back, silently cursing her impatience. He didn't close his eyes this time but touched every millimeter of the paper.

"You see, the threads are too new and strong, and nothing like your father's. On the last one, they'd been so eroded, but I could tell it was your father's signature." He turned silent for a few minutes, then continued. "Ah! Got it. I know where they all are, and there are four of them, but he's changed them all. He went through his To Do List while planting this clue. The only thing of consequence is reporting back to his boss." His eyes flew open and his hands dropped to his sides. "That son of a bitch."

"What? What is it?" As if she hadn't grown a hundred gray hairs already from the stress. His reaction wasn't helping matters any.

"Come on. This bit of information is best told away from here. Trust me." He grabbed her hand and pulled her back toward the exit.

"That bad?"

"Yes, that bad."

"Shit," she muttered as she let herself be led out of the animal park. *Now what?* What could he possibly have learned from the fake note? "Look. I think there's an open bench over by that group of palm trees. Please, I can't wait. Let's go over there and you can tell me what you've found."

"Fine," he grumbled. "But remember, I wanted to do this privately."

"Okay, okay." She hurried them over to a partially isolated bench surrounded by shrubs and palm trees. The fronds gave them some relief from the strong rays of the sun, but when she sat down, the warmth of the baking bench seeped through her pants. "Well?"

He stared at her and took her hands in his own, caressing them gently, soothingly. "I know who's after the Elixxir and who's trying to kill you. In fact, I believe it to be the same person who killed both of your parents."

"That's great! I mean it's not great that someone's trying to kill me, but it's great that you know." Nervous as hell, her heart pounded through her chest. The hand massaging did nothing to allay her uneasiness. Butterflies still fought for freedom from her stomach.

"All right, out with it already!"

"I'm so sorry. It's Eddie Murati."

Stunned, all she could do was blink blindly for a couple of moments. Then, she came to her senses and decided to tell him her opinion of his conclusion. "That's preposterous. You're wrong."

"No, I'm not. I sensed it clearly. The guy was headed back to Murati's Curiosity Shop when he finished placing all the fake clues. And there's another distinct sensory signature on the paper from the guy who wrote it. It's laced with murderous intent, memories of a double murder, and images of a young girl. The paper itself contains threads of pure evil. I'm convinced it's Eddie Murati and that he's fallen under the hand of Satan."

Sweat beaded above her lip. Although the heat of the day seared her skin, a cold chill fired through every nerve-ending, making her shiver involuntarily. Her stomach roiled and her mouth watered, not from the thought or smell of delectable treats, but from the nausea that threatened to conquer her reserve.

"You're wrong. You've got to be wrong. Uncle Eddie wouldn't kill my parents. He wouldn't try to kill me." With her head spinning out of control, she couldn't fight the waves of sickness any longer. She jumped up, turning toward the bushes, and retched. On hands and knees, she continued until there was nothing left inside her. Physically or emotionally. Her gas tank read empty.

Strong yet tender hands grasped her arms, and she leaned into Nathanael as he guided her back to the bench. "Here, take a swig of water and rinse out your mouth."

After pouring some onto a bandana, he handed her the bottle. Then, he took the wet rag and wiped down her face, just like her mother used to do when she was sick. She sipped a bit of water, swished it around her mouth, and spat. But it did little to clean away the vile taste of betrayal and utter disappointment in someone she regarded as family.

Nathanael didn't speak. He didn't try to comfort. He simply kept his distance. It was as if he knew exactly what she needed: space and time to absorb it all. How did one reconcile the duplicity of one who had been so near and dear? She rubbed absently at her heart. It literally ached. All these years she'd been pining away for a chance to reconnect with the only family she had left. And now, to know he had been the one to cause the cataclysmic change in her life shook her to her very core.

A strong breeze stirred, whipping her hair across her cheeks, temporarily cloaking her face from view. Underneath, her disposition changed. And when the wind blew the curtain of hair aside, she looked at Nathanael with a new resolve, a new sense of purpose and determination. She would turn the tables on dear Uncle Eddie and personally rip his life to shreds piece by piece. Until there was nothing left but to rot in jail forever.

Chapter Twelve

*I*f mere intention alone could kill, Nathanael knew Ariana just handed Eddie Murati a death sentence. Her leg had brushed against his ever so briefly, and then she leaned against him, allowing him a glimpse into her state of mind. It was not a pretty place at the moment. He completely understood. He'd been there himself a time or two over the millennia. The hardest lesson to learn in life, no matter how long the life, was the idea that you couldn't trust most people. Unfortunately, she'd been given that lesson more times than he cared to count, and he'd exposed the last link to her past as a fraud and a murderer. No soothing or comforting words would make the news any easier, so he sat there and watched her carefully.

"Let's get the hell out of here, Nate."

"Okay. Where do you want to go?"

"I don't know. Sounds as though Uncle Eddie has the Elixxir at this point. I believe a visit to his shop is in order, to be certain."

"I'll take Gabriel with me. You are most definitely hanging back until we have conclusive evidence that he's our man. Please don't argue with me on this. The Brethren have our ways, and we can keep emotion out of it. I have a plan."

"For now, maybe that's for the best. I'll stay in our room while you go about your business. I honestly don't trust myself not to kill him if I see him. That won't serve us at all in finding the flask."

"Now you're thinking like a soldier! Okay, I'll call Gabriel and have him meet us back at the hotel. Let's go."

She smirked and headed to his bike.

೦೩

Gabriel, Yofi, and Nathanael arrived in a limo, shielding their true identities, at Murati's Curiosity Shop. Gabriel took on the role, as only he could, of a wealthy businessman with money to burn, while Nathanael and Yofi played up their assets as his bodyguards. The two made quite a show of Gabriel's arrival for a couple nosy onlookers by getting out of the car and walking around to open his door. The trainee took a visual sweep of the area. With the coast clear, he ushered Gabriel, wearing his finest navy blue Armani suit, into the store. A bell announced their presence.

Yofi, with his mile-wide shoulders and bulging muscles, made a perfect sentry and stood watch outside the door. As the latest addition to the Brethren Warriors, he impressed Nathanael. He seemed to be a good listener and knew the rudimentary skills necessary for the job. Nothing like the immersion process, though, to see if he could stand up to the rigors of Brethren life.

"Good afternoon, gentlemen. May I help you?"

A tiny, silver-haired lady with the delicate voice of a young child appeared from behind the cash register and smiled.

"Good afternoon, ma'am." Nathanael and Gabriel sauntered up to the counter. "Mr. Lamb here, of Lamb Oil, has been looking for a very specific, shall we say, oddity, and this store came highly recommended. He hopes you can come through for him. Mr. Lamb?"

"Yes, thank you, Miles. I am looking for a piece that is one of only two known in the world. It is a piece from ancient Gaul. A Hadrian votive statuette. Stands about five inches tall."

"Hmm, I know we don't currently have anything like that here, but maybe you should speak with the owner of the shop, Mr. Murati. He's occasionally called upon to seek out odd or rare pieces for customers. Let me tell him you're here first, Mr. Lamb, and see if he's available. Excuse me."

The pixie of a woman shuffled out from behind the counter to a door, with a painted sign that read OFFICE, way in the back of the store. It took her quite a few minutes to get there, and Nathanael stood, shaking his head and pinching the bridge of his nose. Gabriel nudged him and gave an amused look.

"Don't get me started, brother. Once you get me started, I won't be able to stop."

"What? I didn't say anything!" Gabriel played innocent.

"You didn't have to. Your smile said it all. This is serious business. So don't even think about putting the words old woman, antique, and shelf together in a sentence, okay?"

"Okay, I won't say a word. I'll just think it. Actually, she kinda reminds me of one of your grammies from long ago. I'm thinking Middle Ages?"

"You know, you're right. Grammie Aggie. Man, I loved her. What a soft-spoken old lady, but a spitfire when you crossed her. How the heck did you remember that? You were barely here during that time period."

"I guess she made an impression on me. Nothing much else did. No, this current time is exactly what I've been waiting for. Hey, she's coming back."

The woman stopped after a few feet and waved them toward her. "Gentlemen, come to Mr. Murati's office. He has a few minutes to speak with you. Just knock on the door."

"Thank you so much."

They were able to make it to the office and knock before the little old lady made it back to her counter.

"Come in," a deep voice from behind the door called.

Nathanael opened the door and let Gabriel walk in. A quick

look around surprised him. He'd expected a cluttered space filled with bizarre objects and what-nots. But it wasn't like that at all. There were two chairs facing Murati's desk and a framed lithograph of a Monet painting hanging on the wall to the right. That was all. Curious.

"Have a seat, please." He cleared his throat. "What can I do for you today...?" He looked at Nathanael, and then his regard settled on Gabriel, perusing the suit and the Rolex on his wrist.

"Lamb. Austin Lamb of Lamb Oil. I'm in search of an odd piece, a relic, if you will, of which there are only two in existence. It's a Hadrian votive statuette. From ancient Gaul. I'm told you are the man to see when finding what you want proves difficult."

Murati raised his eyebrows. "I see, Mr. Lamb. The search for a piece such as this can take quite a while and include extreme measures. And then, in the end, the piece might be difficult to acquire."

"Money is no object, but I do know what this kind of search entails. So I would say name your fee, within reason, and then we'll talk."

Greed flashed across Murati's face as he figured numbers on his notepad. "I require a retainer of this much. No time limit due to the difficult nature of the search. When I retrieve the piece for you, I will figure its value and let you know." He folded the notepaper and pushed it toward Gabriel.

He, in turn, took the paper and looked at the amount. He didn't flinch, but looked up at Murati. "Agree to half up front, the other half when it's found, and you have a deal."

"Deal."

"Let's shake on it, then, and you can draw up the paperwork." Gabriel extended a hand to him, and the Brethren watched as Murati came out from behind his desk to take it in a hearty handshake.

Nathanael extended his, as well, and Murati hesitated.

"I don't conduct any business without my man here. Shake with him or there is no deal."

He cautiously clasped the Warrior's hand. When they

connected, Nathanael quickly ascertained that his suspicions were correct. All of them. He alerted the other Brethren telepathically and just about had the information on the Elixxir's whereabouts when he sensed something disturbing and evil. Thick, oily goo teased at his shields, while an instantaneous pressure squeezed his hand. Suddenly, Murati's mind closed and locked up tighter than Fort Knox. A red glimmer flashed deep within his eyes, and told him Satan had taken hold.

"So it's the Hadrian you're after?" he asked with a suspicious tone, and clung to the Warrior's hand.

"Yes."

"Nothing else?"

"Maybe after you retrieve this for us we'll consider you for another piece." Nathanael's tracking threads exchanged tugs of war with Murati's possessed soul, with each trying to reveal the other's secrets. But neither would budge an inch or give anything away.

Gabriel stepped toward them after an uncomfortable silence descended upon them. At the very same time, Yofi entered the office. With two massive angels now flanking Murati, and Nathanael nearly crushing his hand, the older and diminutive man slowly backed down and eased the pressure on Nathanael's.

"Everything all right in here, boss?" Yofi frowned and took an imposing stance over the salesman.

"Yes, everything is fine. I'll leave a check with the lovely woman at the counter, Mr. Murati. We'll be in touch. I like to keep a close eye on my investments. In a tangential way, you're one of them." Gabriel turned to leave. "Gentlemen, let's go."

Once outside the shop, Nathanael moved the limo to an inconspicuous corner and reviewed next steps. "Gabriel, we can't leave here. We have to track him. Otherwise we'll never find the flask. Damn it!" He punched the armrest.

"What happened back there? It all seemed to be going fine. You were feeding us good information and then, all of a sudden, nothing."

"Murati is evil on his own, but Satan's gotten to him. I saw the red glow in his eyes for the briefest of moments. He shut him down. I couldn't get anything about where the Elixxir is hidden. But he's definitely got it."

"So now what do we do? Split up? One of us follows him while the others look through his store?"

"Yofi, I'm impressed, man. That's one way to play it out."

"If he's got it in there right now, you know he's gonna take it with him when he leaves."

"Guys, there's something else. I detected something in him that has me very concerned."

"What is it?"

"The Elixxir."

"What? Are you saying he drank the stuff?" Gabriel scooted to the edge of his seat. "Shit! If you're right then I have some heavy research to do on how to kill someone who's taken from the flask."

"Immortality and evil possession. Not a good mix. Remember that, Yofi."

"Got it." He took out a little notepad and started writing, then stopped. "But he looks old, guys. I thought the Elixxir gave a person immortality."

"It does, at the age-point it's taken. He's never going to age beyond what he is right now. But it doesn't make him any less dangerous. He's immortal now. And he's Satan's puppet."

"Shit. Hey, we didn't leave a deposit for the fake search! Nathanael, go back inside with this and see if you can get any more information." Gabriel handed him a checkbook.

"Okay. Be right back. Hey, wait. Yofi, raise your shields and go in with me. You can hang out in there and keep a real close eye on things."

"Got it."

He liked second chances. And he would do his damnedest to make this one pay off.

Waiting around was not a strong suit of hers. Why Ariana had agreed to stay back and didn't fight to go along, she didn't know. Maybe the shock of it all had numbed her brain. She paid the price for that now. Impatience ate away at her control like a flesh-eating virus. She had to do something or she would explode. Uncle Eddie had killed her parents and had wanted her dead for twenty years. Time to start ripping his life to shreds right under his nose, and without him realizing it.

She knew her way around computers and the Internet a bit, using it all the time at the tour company. If she could get into Murati's store and on to his computer, she could do some major, irreparable damage. Embezzlement, maybe? Tie him to organized crime? Oh yes, she could have a grand time! Itching to get started, she grabbed her bag and rushed out of the room.

Once downstairs, she bought herself a big T-shirt, bug-eyed sunglasses, and a floppy sunhat. She put her hair up in a bun and the items she bought did the rest to conceal her identity. Next, she hired a cab before any second thoughts could creep into her brain. The Brethren were all over the Elixxir angle. Good for them. But all they wanted was to retrieve the flask. She would have her revenge, and it would be sweet. Her knee bobbed furiously up and down as the cab pulled to a stop in front of the store. Doubt seeped into her plans and she sat frozen in her seat.

What the hell do you think you're doing? What if the Brethren are still inside? What if Murati is inside? She took a look out the windows at the cars parked along the street. No one sat waiting in them.

"Hey lady, we're here."

"Could you wait for me, please? Here's what I owe you for the ride so far. I'll pay you for waiting and the trip back to the hotel when I come back. Okay?"

"Yeah, sure. It's your dime."

He took the twenty she handed him. "Keep the change, and don't move. Please." The driver grumbled something unintelligible.

She opened the car door and scanned the area. All looked

clear. *It's now or never, girlie. Got your balls strapped on? Check. Then let's go ruin a life that ain't worth livin'.* She took a deep breath, got out of the car, and marched into the store. As the door closed behind her and hit her in the butt, she stood transfixed, immediately thrown back to her childhood days.

She kept her sunglasses on in the dimly lit store. Everything looked the same! After all this time, as she scanned the stock on the shelves, nothing had changed! The monkey claws were on the same shelf. Right between the glass eyes and the skeletons of small animals. The furnishings hadn't been updated, nor the layout of the place. The ticking of a grandfather clock rustled up a faded bit of memory regarding a hide-and-seek game she used to play. Even the musty smell that she loved as a child remained, only now, it choked her. She coughed and tried breathing through her mouth.

"Good afternoon, young lady. May I help you find something?"

Jesus! This lady is probably as old as.... Oh, my God! It can't be. Grammie Murati? She's still alive?

"Miss, if you have something in mind, I can help you."

"I...uh...well. Yes, can you help me find a mummified cat, please?" It was the first thing that came to mind.

"Of course. We keep those way in the back. If you'd like to join me...."

"I think I'll look around these aisles here, if you don't mind. Pick the cat that's in the best condition for me."

"Okay, then. I'll be right back." The old woman hobbled out from behind the cashier's counter and made her way to the Egyptian Oddities section of the store.

Ariana scanned to see if the store's video surveillance cameras still hung where they had twenty years ago. Dust and all, they were still there. She took out her foam antibacterial hand sanitizer, ambled nonchalantly toward and under the one focused on the checkout counter and sprayed a good dose in the lens. She wouldn't have much time to scurry over to the computer and look for what she wanted. The items in the store hadn't changed at all, and neither had Murati's bookkeeping. She sneaked behind the counter and sat down in front of the keyboard. Grammie had forgotten to log out before going on her cat hunt, making quick work to find the files Ariana needed.

A click here, a click there, transferring money from one bank account to another. Switching things around in an Excel spreadsheet took mere moments to accomplish. The hard part entailed linking those changes to Murati's bank account so it looked like he'd stolen from his own store. She needed a Social Security number to complete the transaction. Where the heck was she going to find that? She hoped Grammie would be indecisive about which cat to bring up to the front.

Clicking at the speed of light, she searched through files in the hopes of finding one with those nine golden numbers. Aha! A tax form!

A wobbly voice called in the distance. "I think I found you the perfect cat, miss."

Scrambling to finish, Ariana's fingers flew over the keyboard and hit enter. At the last moment, she remembered to return the screen to its original view and scurried back around the counter just as Grammie came into view. Breathing heavily, she willed herself to calm down.

"Wonderful, thank you!" She smiled broadly.

By the time the woman and the cat made it to the front of the store her normal breath had returned. But frenetic nerve-endings still fired prickly sensations across her skin. She had to get out of there before Murati made an appearance. She couldn't stop glancing over at the office door, swearing that at any moment it would open and he would come walking out, see her, and kill her on the spot. The killing her on the spot part took her delusion a little too far, but her perspective was way off at this point.

"Now isn't this a lovely piece?" Grammie set the mummy down on the counter.

"Yes, I'll take it. How much?"

"That'll be three hundred dollars."

"Whoa! Too rich for my blood. But thank you for finding such a beautiful specimen. Oh, I'm late for an appointment! Gotta run. Have a good day." She hurried out of the shop, straight into the waiting cab.

"Back to the hotel, please, quickly."

"Sure thing."

She looked out the back window as the cab pulled away. The door opened abruptly and a gray-haired man rushed out, looking first to his left, then to his right and settled on her cab nearing the end of the block. His gaze locked on to hers for the briefest of moments. A smug grin on his face said it all. She turned around frantically and ducked down low in her seat. Her heart pounded out a rhythm in time with a word repeating in her head—*stupid*—and she gasped for air. Uncle Eddie.

"You all right there, lady?"

"Fine. Just leave as fast as you can." She clutched at her chest and held on to the door handle, trying to get hold of herself and sanity. Step one had been completed. Step two.... Did she even have a step two? *Call the Feds anonymously and report embezzlement on Uncle Eddie's part. That's step two.* She prayed the Brethren hadn't returned yet from their expedition. But if they were sitting in her room right now, she'd have to have a good story lined up.

After paying the cab driver, she hustled over to the hotel spa. That would be a logical place to hang out while the angels played. Stress demanded she find an outlet. She stripped and put her things in a locker. Wrapped in a towel, she headed for the steam room. She'd stay there for a while and then head back to the room. Of course, Nathanael would be upset not to find her there, but what did he expect her to do? They'd exchanged cell phone numbers, so if he really needed to get ahold of her, he could call. Not that she'd be able to answer the phone, since it was in her locker. But these were the things that made it easy for her to lie about where she'd truly been.

ଔ

Nathanael trudged out of the store, for the second time that day, with a huge scowl on his face and joined Gabriel in the limo. "Satan's cloaked him, Gabe," he said quietly. "Granny in there said he wasn't in his office. Must've left and forgot to tell her. Stupid on my part not to think he wouldn't be able to cloak. He could still be in there or not, and we wouldn't know."

"With Yofi shielded in there, too, we'll get some answers. He's good."

"I hope so. I gotta get back to Ariana. I don't want her left alone any longer than she needs to be. She's still got a mark on her, and I'm not gonna let her die on my watch."

"Think I'll stay and take to the rooftops to keep watch. I'll keep you updated."

"Thanks, man."

Gabriel shielded, and left Nathanael driving back with plenty to think about. His thoughts went immediately to the woman waiting for him in their room. He took out his cell phone and called her. It went straight to voicemail.

Chapter Thirteen

She'd first thought of it as just a viable alibi, but the steam room worked its magic on Ariana's frayed nerves. As minutes ticked on by, the steamy tendrils eased their way into her tense muscles. For the first time in a long while, she let her walls lower and stopped thinking about everything except how wonderful the warm, moist air soothed her skin and soul. She must have dozed off for a few minutes because her eyelids fluttered open unexpectedly. Feeling like a sopping mess of a wet rag, she decided enough time had probably passed to head on upstairs.

More steam seemed to be pumping through the pipes than when she'd first entered the room, and it had become a bit uncomfortable. She bounced to her feet and fell right back down. Overcome by a wave of dizziness, she'd forgotten to take her time when getting up. She closed her eyes for a minute. When she stood up the next time, she took it nice and easy. As she pushed on the door, she nearly crashed her head into it. It didn't open. She pushed again. It wouldn't budge. She took a deep breath and shoved it with her shoulder.

Damn it! Now what should I do?

She banged hard with her fists and shouted at the top of her lungs. After a few minutes and nobody coming, she did it again. The steam had gotten really thick, making it difficult to see even past her face, let alone trying to find the thermostat control. Panic replaced the calm. She pounded on the door until her knuckles were bright red and throbbing. She screamed until her voice gave out. Nobody answered, and the door hadn't moved a millimeter.

The increased moisture caused labored and shallow breathing, as though she drank air. Limbs deadened from exhaustion and the room swirled around her. She imagined herself broccoli cooking in the largest steam-cooker known to man. She laughed deliriously, and then gave the door a shove with the last bit of energy she had left. Fear overwhelmed her as she slid down the glass insert and sank to the floor.

"Nathanael, help me...." She sobbed quietly as the world faded to black.

After dropping off the limo with valet parking, Nathanael raced into the hotel, anxious to see Ariana again. He could fool himself into thinking it was only to see that she was safe. But he was no fool. He missed her voice, her spunk, her body. It only made him walk that much faster to the elevator. The door opened, and he stepped inside. Anticipation raced through his veins, making his heart race. The same rapid pace as when he prepared for a bounty pickup or a battle. He hoped she'd be willing to oblige his pent-up energy as she had last night.

Absently, he looked around the empty elevator car and fantasized different scenarios that they could act out from lobby to penthouse. Suddenly, his senses exploded with intense fear, heat, and despair. He grabbed hold of the railing to keep steady. A vision of thick fog clouded his eyes and a voice called out to him for help. *Ariana.* She's in danger! But where? Intense heat, steam.... Is she in the shower? No. He fought for more direction from his senses. He saw a door with the hotel insignia etched on the front. The steam room!

He immediately pushed the button to stop on the next floor. As the doors opened, he raced out, pulled off his T-shirt, and flung himself down the stairwell as his wings unfurled. Before entering the lobby, he put his shirt back on and ran to the spa. A woman sat behind the sign-in counter, her back facing him.

"Excuse me, where's the steam room?" She didn't turn around or answer him. "I said where is the steam room, ma'am?" He reached over and touched her shoulder. She slumped over, revealing a small welt on her neck, most likely from a syringe. He pressed a finger to check for a pulse. She had one, so he ventured on in search of Ariana.

A right turn and a left, and the room lay straight ahead. He ran over and saw a figure slouched against the door. Someone had wedged a bar so the door couldn't open. He ripped the bar out and although he wanted to fling the door open, he slowly pulled it so as not to injure the person any further.

Ariana lay in a heaping mass, unconscious. He picked her up, and sat down on a bench to look her over. Pinkish-red skin felt hot to the touch. Pulse was erratic and breathing shallow. She needed to be cooled down fast, so he brought her into one of the shower stalls. The cold water rained upon the both of them. He hoped it would be all she needed. A few minutes passed and she stirred a little in his arms.

"Ariana? Red, can you hear me?" He swiped at the water cascading down the side of her face and cupped her cheek. "Come on, girl. Wake up for me."

"So hot...." she murmured.

"I know, I know. I'm cooling you down right now. Just stay with me, okay?"

"Nate...."

"I'm here, Red. I'm here." He kissed her forehead and nuzzled her hair.

"The door...I couldn't open it."

"I know, baby."

"I called...to you." She whimpered and his heart ached. "You came."

He held her closer. "I'll always come for you." She shivered.

He raised an arm to turn off the cold water. After toweling her dry, he found complimentary robes hanging and wrapped one around her. Not wanting to get associated with any trouble surrounding the drugged receptionist, he opted for shielding the two of them until they were back in their room.

When he rested her on the bed, she seemed more alert. "How are you doing? Any better?"

"I feel like crap, but I'll live. Thanks to you." She smiled weakly.

"Thanks to me, you were left alone and nearly died." He scoffed, took the notepad from the bedside table, and threw it against the wall. Sitting down beside her, he said, "Never again. I don't go anywhere without you, and you don't go anywhere without me. Not until Murati and his men are caught and dealt with."

"You had a job to do, Nate. And it had to do with me. I couldn't stand being cooped up in here any longer and went down to the steam room. I put myself in danger by staying in there too long and not having enough strength to open the freakin' door."

"You're right. You were foolish for leaving the room. And I could kill ya for that. But you weren't too weak. Someone deliberately drugged the receptionist, jammed the door shut so it couldn't open, and turned the thermostat all the way up. How the hell did he find you here? That's what I want to know." Ariana shifted in bed and coughed. He raked his hand through his hair, completely frustrated. "Shit, maybe when we shook hands he read me the way I read him. Damn it. Gabriel needs to give us protections."

"What the heck are you talking about?"

"Murati's possessed, which leaves him open as a conduit for Satan."

"Possessed by Satan? Seriously?" She looked dubious.

"Yes, I'm deadly serious. Just like those men at the bus station." He rested a hand on her arm.

She fidgeted and settled on her side. "The only good thing about all of this is that he probably believes you're dead at this point. We can exploit that. But that's not for you to think about."

He got up. "For now, rest and recover."

"Where are you going?" Her hand shot out and grabbed at his leg, but her panicked voice sat him back down immediately.

"I need to change out of my wet clothes and then I'll sit in the chair so you can sleep," he said softly. She shook her head and her frantic eyes rocked him to his core.

"No! I don't want to sleep. I don't want to rest or close my eyes. Show me I'm alive, Nate."

She'd escaped death's grip more times than she cared to count. There were only so many times a person could nearly die before they started getting a complex. She had no intention of leaving this earth any time soon, but these accumulated occurrences couldn't be ignored.

"I'm afraid one of these days you're gonna be too late to save me. Show me what I've got to fight to my dying breath for."

Ariana opened her robe and exposed more than her vulnerability. Nathanael looked as though he would protest, but then his scrutiny traversed the length of her, and when his eyes rested once again upon hers, they told a different story.

He shucked his soggy T-shirt and his wings fluttered out. "Will this do?" Unbuttoning his fly, he'd gone commando and now stood at attention. She smiled, but before she could comment, his pants and boots were gone, socks flung to corners of the room. He stood with arms open wide, offering himself in all his splendid, angelic glory. She raised her hand and grabbed his.

"Come here, and I'll tell you."

He didn't resist her tugging at him, but instead eased himself on top of her so their bodies touched lightly. Breathing hotly against her lips and caressing her cheeks with the backs of his hands, he whispered, "How about now?"

She wound her fingers through his mass of damp hair and closed the distance between them. His mouth, all soft and warm, opened to her demands, and he met her urgency with his own. He nipped at her bottom lip then soothed it with his tongue. She groaned with need. He pulled back slightly, raising a questioning brow.

"More," she demanded.

"Oh, there's much more I have in store for you." With his fingers, he traced a path along the side of her breast to her waist. Goosebumps rose and tiny chills danced across her skin. "Ariana, you are the most alive person I know. This mess will all be over soon and you can be yourself, out loud and proud, without any more threats."

"I want that so much." She really did, but if he didn't step things up, she knew she would explode. Taking matters into her own hands—taking him into her hands—she conveyed without words what she wanted.

Nathanael sucked air in through his gritted teeth and crushed his lips against hers for a soul-stealing kiss. She ground her hips against him, toying with the idea of making this time hard and fast. His hands teased their way up and down her body. And when he finally let go of her mouth, he blazed new trails, stopping to nuzzle each breast, massaging each with his tongue.

She'd been craving this kind of bliss, and explored her angel's massive body with the same fervor. His smooth, slick skin barely contained muscles that quivered underneath from her touch. She equated him to a nuclear reactor headed for a meltdown, and she planned on being right there with him when he did.

Feathers shimmered in the fading sunlight as the setting sun peeked through the curtains and cast a golden glow over his body. Mesmerized, she had to touch those wings again. Reaching out, she saw them tremble around her, as though they sensed her approach. She decided to be a little devilish and, with her touch, bring him to the brink of rapture. Light swipes and flicks to different areas of his wings brought about spasms that wracked his entire body. He cried out while clutching her fiercely to him, and she smiled deep inside, completely satisfied knowing she'd brought this kind of pleasure to him.

But another kind of release begged to be set free, and

Nathanael's heated gaze told her she'd play a major part in that. She met him with boldness, and winked. He smiled back and rubbed his hands from her shoulders down to her wrists. As he made the return trip, he lifted her arms to rest above her head. He rose above her and kissed each palm delicately, then continued to feather kisses lightly down one arm until he met her neck, where he suckled and flicked his tongue. Her arms involuntarily lowered a bit, but he returned them to their position and worked his way down her body, inch by excruciating inch. No spot remained untouched by his hands, his lips, or his tongue.

"You taste so good." He'd returned his attentions to her ear and growled softly. "Like ambrosia, you are. Food of the gods. I can't get enough of you." He gathered her up in his arms and pressed his need against her. "I'll have you for breakfast, lunch, and dinner."

"Have me now." She opened for him, grabbed his muscled ass, and guided him inside her.

How had she ever lived before this? Making love with Nathanael went beyond any fantasies she'd dreamt of, and those usually came from romance novels anyway. As he glided and thrust in and out of her, she felt complete and bereft, turn for turn. He quickened the pace and the tingling low in her body grew exponentially until she lost all sense of time and place. All thought left her and only sensation remained until at last, she shuddered and climaxed with him a moment later. He collapsed on top of her. Managing to stay inside, he rolled onto his back, bringing her atop to ride out the remaining waves of ecstasy.

"Miss Ariana Kupi," he said, and kissed the top of her head. "I declare you very much alive."

"Are you sure?" She cuddled closer. "Because I think I died and went to heaven."

A low rumble of laughter shook her and she nearly teetered off of him. But he secured her in place, and they spent a good, long while in contented silence. As her body cooled, she realized all of her things were still at the spa. Her bag, her phone, her clothes, her disguise. How would she get them back? She lifted her head up and looked at her warrior.

"Nate, my stuff is still in the spa locker. I need to get it back."

"We can go together. I'll shield us. Remember, tied at the hip. You and me." He grabbed her around her waist and gave a little thrust.

"Mmmm. Yeah, I got that memo. Here's my response." She pushed herself up and sat astride, laughing and ready for more of what her angel had in store.

ભ

Shielding and getting them both back to the spa was the easy part. Opening the locker proved difficult. There were cops everywhere, but no sign of the receptionist. They'd have to wait for them to clear out of the locker room area before he allowed Ariana inside.

"What are we waiting for? The locker is right here in front of us," she whispered in his ear.

It sent shivers down his spine and he frowned at her. "Hey, stop doing that. I'm already keyed up from seeing all the cops here. I don't need you sending me over the edge. And by the way, you don't have to whisper. As long as you're holding on to me, everything about us is cloaked."

"Sorry, I didn't know. So why are we waiting? If you can cloak everything you touch...."

"Yeah, well, nothing's perfect and I don't want the entire police force puzzling over why a particular locker area looks funky. It shouldn't be too much longer. I heard a couple of them talking and one said they should be home in time for dinner."

"Speaking of dinner...I'm starving! Can we get something after we get my stuff?"

"Sure. I'm sorry. I'm used to going for hours and hours without food, so I tend to forget about others' eating habits."

"Hey, they're leaving. Look." She pointed to the throng of police making their way out of the spa.

"Perfect. Now we make our move." He leaned his hand against the door. "Open it."

"Wait a minute." She stood there for a moment with a puzzled look on her face and then smiled. "Okay, I remember the number sequence. Whew!"

With a couple of punches on a keypad, the door clicked open and she began to take out her belongings.

"Hey. When did you get this?" He reached in and pulled out a floppy hat.

"Oh, I bought it earlier at one of the gift shops. Can I have it, please?" She made a grab for it a little too quickly for his liking and he snatched it away before she succeeded.

"That's okay. I'll hold it while you get the rest of your things out." He thought he saw a bit of trepidation on her face and watched as she pulled out the rest of the items from the locker. As she did so, he let his senses do the walking all over the hat. It wasn't that he didn't trust her, but he didn't...trust anyone. What had she done while he was away?

She went out. There's tension here. Holy shit, she went to Murati's Curiosity Shop! Why the hell did she do that? And when? While we were there, we didn't see her or anyone come through the door. There's more. She intends to bring Murati down and laid the groundwork while she visited there. Satisfaction. Mmmm. And fear. Son of a bitch! He saw her.

"Are you insane, woman? Isn't it bad enough that Murati wants you out of the picture? Oh no, you have to go and give yourself to him on a silver platter!" He fumed, and forgetting all about the shielding, he let go of her to scrub his face, rendering them both visible and audible to the world. He slammed his hand against the metal locker, denting it.

She shrank back and winced.

"Damn it! Why couldn't you stay in the room like a good girl, like a reasonable woman, like I told you? You had me thinking the whole time that it was my fault you nearly got killed today. Mine! When all the time you knew your inability to control your impulses was really to blame. Do you really want to live, Ariana?

Because I'm getting the distinct impression here that you don't."

He paced like a lion ready to pounce on his prey, while a bullet train of energy coursed through his veins. If he didn't leave now, he would destroy the room. And he didn't know if he could protect her from his rage.

She didn't say a word. She just stood there, shrinking more and more into the wall with a look of utter shock and guilt on her face. But he couldn't stop himself.

"Take your stuff and go back to the room. Or don't. I'm getting the fuck out of here." He threw the hat on the floor and left her where she stood. He didn't know where to go, but bad guys were gonna fall tonight.

Ariana stood, stupefied. He'd held her hat and found out what she'd done. She deserved everything he'd said. All of it. And more. How would she ever make this up to him? An apology seemed inadequate. Looking back, she'd put the whole operation in jeopardy with her silly notion of bringing Uncle Eddie down by herself. She didn't consider the consequences of her actions with regards to the Elixxir and the Brethren. What if she'd blown the whole thing to smithereens? Could she be sent to Hell for this?

"Are you all right, dearie?" Two elderly women with concerned looks on their faces shuffled over to her. One rested a hand on her arm. "We were walking by when we saw that big brute of a man yell at you and blast his way out of here. He didn't hurt you, did he? We could get the police for you."

"No! No, he didn't hurt me. And his bark is worse than his bite. It's really my fault he's so angry. But thank you. I appreciate you coming over and checking. I'm gonna go up to the room now. I think that's enough excitement for one day." She patted the woman's hand and smiled as she left the two to their inevitable prattle.

That's where I should have been all along.

Chapter Fourteen

*T*he sun had set a couple of hours ago and Ariana had shredded a whole box of tissues with worry over her angel's state of mind. He hadn't called or been back since the debacle in the spa. She'd ordered room service when she'd gotten back upstairs, but it sat, mostly untouched. After mutilating the last napkin, she opted for strangling a hand towel while pacing the floor.

Voices in the hall had her on alert, and then a knock on the door sent her scrambling to the bathroom to hide.

"Hey, Nathanael! It's Gabriel and Yofi. Open up."

Feeling like a fool, she got out of the tub, unlocked the bathroom door, and opened the room's door to awaiting angels. "Hi, come in. Nate's not here at the moment." She closed the door and continued. "I'm Ariana."

"Yes, we know. I'm Gabriel. This is Yofi. We're colleagues of Nathanael's."

"I know all about it, Gabriel. You don't have to pretend around me. Congrats on the new job, Yofi."

The Brethren looked at each other and back at her. "What exactly do you know?"

"You're angels and you fight Evil while protecting us humans. Don't worry about me knowing, though. Raphael and

139

Serena are close friends of mine, and your buddy, Kemuel, and I were a thing a ways back. Not anymore, though, so make sure you remember that. Anyway, your buddy's not here, and I don't know when he's gonna be back because he's gone MIA, probably looking for all kinds of trouble, thanks to me." She took a breath and took a drink of water.

The two behemoths, one in a suit and the other in leather pants and T-shirt, sat down on the bed looking none too pleased.

"Okay. Start talking. What happened?"

ಡಿ

Nathanael rode his Harley hard around Las Vegas looking for the seediest parts of town. Evil would pay heavily tonight. He stopped in front of a dive bar down some street he didn't even know. Men stood outside smoking cigarettes and joints, talking trash about women. In the bar, he could hear others arguing over how to tell the difference between a "he/she" and a real woman. He drove on.

After countless turns and stops he finally came across a convenience store. Its occupants were currently robbing the place at gunpoint. He swaggered through the door to the chorus of screams from the clerks. One of the robbers turned his gun on him.

"Hey, man! Keep on walking and empty your pockets on the counter. Now!"

"I don't think so, asswipe." Nathanael kept walking toward the man. Disregarding the bullets making holes in his T-shirt, he punched him square in the jaw and grabbed the gun out of his hand. He punched him a second time and smiled as he watched him slump to the floor.

"What the fuck?" The second man stalked over with his semi-automatic pointing straight at the Brethren's heart. "I'm gonna make you wish you were never born, asshole."

"And I'll make sure history *shows* you never were."

The Warrior taunted and waved him to approach. Instead,

the thief chose to charge him and unload his magazine. Bullets shredded the remaining bits of his T-shirt and were quickly absorbed into his skin, like the others. Shock and horror washed over the guy's face. In a crazed and desperate move, he tossed the gun at him and backed up.

"Whoa! Whoa! Who the hell are you?"

Nathanael stepped forward, picked up the scrawny cokehead by his neck, and lifted him high in the air with his left hand. "I'm the last one your poor excuse for a life is gonna see before you die and go to Hell. Remember my name when you get there. It's Nathanael. Tell Satan you're number one."

"Wha—" But before the thug could finish his thought, Nathanael unsheathed his sword and threw the man up in the air. As his body descended, the angel pivoted and sliced right through his neck. More screams and shouts erupted as the sales clerks ran out of the store.

The ancient inscription on the sword glowed fiery orange-red, and the blade soaked up the blood that coated the length of it. Nathanael's arms shook violently as electricity shot through every cell of his body. Rapture blinded him and he fell to his knees. Tears streamed down his cheeks. As his adrenaline rush slowly subsided, he hung his head and said, "Now for number two."

೦ಽ

"That was you in the store? I saw you! I was shielded, hoping to find Murati or at least sense where he went and if he took the Elixxir. You were messing with the computer up front while granny was in the back looking for something." Yofi shook his head and laughed.

"Yes, that was me. I'm not ashamed to say I framed him for embezzlement and ran out of there. I'm so sorry if I screwed things up for you. Haven't had a chance to apologize to Nate, though."

"Don't worry, I got the information we need to move

forward."

"You know where the Elixxir is?" Finally, a break for the good guys, Ariana thought.

"Yup. It's with Murati. He's got it in his pocket, and he plans on going to a show this evening."

"So now all we have to do is find Nate and you can get it back from my murdering uncle. Can you figure out where he is?"

"Well, normally, we have open lines of contact between us, but there are times when we put up walls for privacy. He's blocked us. That's why we came all the way here instead of using telepathy."

"Damn it. I'm worried about him." She pounded her fist on the bedside table. "When he left me.... Let me put it to you this way. I wouldn't want to be the fool to cross his path. He could cause some serious damage to a lot of people out there. I'm afraid he's gone on a rage-filled bender."

Gabriel stood, an imposing, towering skyscraper. "What exactly are you saying? You're making him out to be some kind of violence junkie. He's a bounty hunter and a Brethren Warrior. Violence is his job."

"I know, Gabriel. But tell me," she countered, "do the other Warriors get a high when they slice and dice? Do they look for reasons to fight? Do they case the most dangerous parts of town in the hopes of finding someone to pummel into Hell?"

Silence.

"Didn't think so. But Nathanael has. I'll bet you a million dollars he's roaming the streets doing exactly that. Do you know Joe's number?"

"Joe? Who's Joe?"

"You must know Joe. He's his personal fitness trainer and old friend. He's the only one who knows—I mean...he can tell you how serious this is.

"Oh! Joseph Demonico. Yes, I'll have Yofi call him. It would be helpful to know what we're dealing with here."

"Find him, Gabriel. Fly through the night and find him. Then, lock me in a room with him and I'll set him straight. I made this mess and I'll fix it."

"Thanks, but we'll handle it." Gabriel turned to his teammate. "Yofi, we need to call in the others for this. When one of us is hurting, we all are."

"I'll alert them right now. Want me to tell them to meet us on the rooftop here?"

"Yeah, that'll work. But what to do about Murati and the Elixxir? We've got to get that situation neutralized. Let me think on it."

CS

Nathanael checked email through his phone and found a list of bounties to be hunted. The streets of Las Vegas proved too tame for him, and he needed to ramp it up. He called his warden friends and discovered there were four highly dangerous escaped convicts on the loose from different county jails across Arizona and Nevada. He flew to each one and asked for a shirt or something personal from each escapee. He sensed each of their intentions and began his hunt.

He started with a fugitive, Jerry Mack, who'd shot and killed his wife and three kids. He'd escaped an Arizona county jail and had last been seen near Carson City. Lucky Nate. He got to pick off the first one close to home. Jerry had plans to visit Reno. Straight to his other wife and kids who lived there. Fucking polygamist. *Well, not anymore.*

Flying off to where he suspected Jerry would be, his adrenaline started pumping again and his heart thrummed with the thrill that had teased him all evening. Down below, in a little hidey hole at the end of a dark alley, the murderer sat eating chicken wings.

"Enjoying your dinner, Jerry?" Nathanael came to land in front of him. He looked up and dropped the wing that he'd been gnawing on.

"Oh, that look is priceless, Jer, my man. Priceless! Wait, I gotta get a picture of this." He took out his cell phone and pushed the camera button. "Okay, hold it right there. Perfect!" He stowed his cell phone back in his pants pocket. "I'll be sure to send you a copy...in Hell."

"What the fuck are you? Some kind of freak?" He dropped his bag of wings and scooted back against the wall.

"Yeah, I'm the freak here. Uh huh. Let's see, now. You, Jerry Mack, married two women and raised two families at the same time without either knowing about it. You just murdered one of your wives and three of your kids. And I'm the freak? Because of these things, here?" He pointed to his wings.

"I didn't kill nobody."

"You're a fucking liar and a very bad man. Being the angel that I am, I don't take kindly to people who murder innocent children. Now, I could bring you back to jail, but I really don't want to waste taxpayer dollars feeding you and buying toilet paper to wipe your psychopathic ass. No, I'd much rather deliver Brethren justice upon ya."

"You're one sick motherfucker." Jerry pulled out a gun.

"Really? That's all you got? Almost makes this boring. Don't bother to shoot me. I don't die. Now, since you've been on the run from the law, why don't we pick up where you left off."

He gave him a puzzled look.

"That means run, Jerry. Run for your life. Go."

The crazed man scrambled out of the corner and raced away from him. "One, two, three...." Nathanael shuddered, absorbing the high, and flew off after him. He watched him race down an unlit street, giving him plenty of lead time. Almost without effort, he lifted and landed about fifty yards in front of the desperate man. He stood like a massive wall of impenetrable flesh. Jerry stopped short and turned to run the other way. But the Warrior simply flew over and alighted in front of him again.

"Ever play tag when you were a kid? You don't seem to be too good at it." Nathanael's head pounded and he needed release. He flew around the screaming man at lightning speed, and then punched his fist out, knocking him to the ground. "Tag! You're it!"

The dazed man looked up at the avenging angel.

"Jerry Mack, you have been charged with four counts of first-degree murder and one count of escape from jail. How do you plead? This is when you say guilty, Jerry. Go ahead."

"G-g-guilty, all right? Just who the hell are you?"

"I'm your personal Angel of Death. My name is Nathanael, and I will be delivering justice all over your ass tonight. Swiftly and permanently." He unsheathed his sword and watched as it glinted in the moonlight. "Time to go to Hell. Say hi to Satan for me. Tell him you're number two."

He raised his sword and howled as Jerry scurried across the road, trying to get away from him. But Nathanael had other business to attend to and made quick work of his bounty, severing the man's head from his body. The sword shimmered and absorbed the man's blood. Nathanael shrieked from the pain and the pleasure of it all. His arms stretched up to the skies, and he shouted. "Ah! More...I need more!" He flew off to feed on the next loser of a bounty. "Lord, help me stop."

Darkness slid neatly into the recesses of his mind as Satan paid him a visit. "I'm here for you. No one else is. Where's your boss? The coward. Where's your woman? Lying whore. Who's always given you what you need? Me. And I can give you all that and more. Join me, and you can have all the power you desire."

Evil taunted his soul and fueled his skewed thoughts. It massaged his addiction and his ego, but he couldn't seem to jump the last hurdle necessary to become Satan's angel forever. He could not kill for blood-sport.

"No! I will not yield!" He stumbled onward and took flight, needing the wind to rush around him and looking for the next fix.

The second escaped convict had intended to get revenge on an ex-girlfriend who'd turned him into the police. Nathanael touched down right behind Jake Fremont as he took a container of gasoline from the bed of a presumably stolen pick-up truck. Looked like he was planning on torching the house in front of them.

"Jake Fremont!" he whispered ominously in his ear, and then he flew behind a tree.

The guy jumped and spilled the gasoline on his pants. "Shit! What the fuck?" He turned around and around looking like a dog chasing his tail.

"Jake Fremont," Nathanael taunted as he floated down before him, "you are hereby charged with two counts of murder and one count of being a stupid ass for thinking you could escape prison. You are hereby sentenced to Brethren justice. Any last words before you die, you worthless piece of scum?"

"I...I...." Jake stood frozen, and dropped the bottle on the ground.

"I...I...." The Warrior mocked him and unsheathed his sword, waving it about with flair. "I didn't do it? Wrong. It was an accident? No, douchebag, thirty-five stab wounds isn't an accident. Prepare to meet your new prison boyfriend: Satan. And tell him, you're number three."

Jake tried to flee. "You run like a sissy, Fremont!" He flew after him and cut him down mid-stride. The head rolled to the gutter as the rest of the body crumpled like a ragdoll.

"Clean up in Aisle Hell, please." Nathanael let out a maniacal laugh and cried at the same time. "Ah!" He held his head and shook uncontrollably. The ecstasy of the kill collided with the pain of Satan's choking grasp on him.

Evil warred with the good inside him, twisting his innards into knots and gnarled masses, and wouldn't let up. It teased and lapped at his heart and soul, tempting them with ultimate power, leaving behind extreme want and desire. Fire raced through his veins and all the barbs of his feathers. He fell to the ground and picked himself up again, realizing he needed to find a sheltered place to get through this hellish period.

A playground stood halfway down the street, with equipment that could serve to hide him while he went off the deep end. It took every ounce of his will to stumble over to a large cement tube big enough to hold him. He fell into it just as the rapture pushed all sense aside and took total control. His mind fell into the waiting hands of darkness.

Maybe I should finally give in to Satan. I'm tired of feeling this way. Tired of the constant craving and never being satisfied.

He rose to his knees and grasped the sword. With both hands in a death grip around the hilt, he tried to turn the blade inward, ending his piteous existence. But instead, it did what it always did when he tried. It trembled and shook furiously, and then tossed itself out of his hands when he'd managed to get it pointed at his heart.

"Damn you to Hell!" He threw himself to the floor of the tube and curled up in a fetal position as another wave of rapture pulled him under. "Ariana!"

Chapter Fifteen

*A*riana had never felt more shitty in her life. Her impulsivity and lies had sent Nathanael off the deep end. She wanted to scream, wanted to rip her own heart out and smash it to pieces. She had to find him and beg forgiveness, or she'd go nuts herself. The Brethren had long since congregated and flown off blindly to seek him out. Because he blocked them, they could only scan the streets. But who knew where he'd really gone? He could have flown halfway around the world, and no one would know.

Standing by the window, she looked toward the sky and prayed he would find his way back to her. Suddenly, a deep voice called to her from behind, and she turned around sharply. No one was there. She turned again, and an image popped into her head out of nowhere. A deserted playground by her old elementary school. Her pulse quickened as she tried to put sense to the strange events.

The voice sounded familiar, deep and sensual, and desperate, yet no one but she remained in the room, so it couldn't be one of the Brethren. And why would she be thinking about the old playground now? That voice....

"Oh, my God! It's him! It's Nate!"

She hurried to slip on her shoes and grabbed her bag while

running out of the room. Nathanael had called to her and needed her help. She knew it now. If she could get a cab right away, it would take all of five minutes to get there. "I'm coming for you, Nate. Hold on."

CƷ

Ariana barely waited for the cab to come to a full stop before opening the door and running. *The man could be a jungle gym in his own right given how enormous he is. He couldn't be that hard to find.* She ran around until she came to cement tubes she remembered playing in as a child. They were the only things she could think of that were large enough to contain the guy.

"Nathanael? Nate? Where are you?" There were five of these cement behemoths, and she raced from one to the next until she heard grunts of pain and found a curious, flickering glow emanating from the last one. She approached tentatively and looked inside. "Oh, my God."

He lay curled up in a ball. Sandy grit had mixed with his sweat and caked on his wings and arms. Tremors wracked his entire body and she could hear him mumbling something unintelligible over and over.

"Nathanael," she whispered, and crouched low in front of him. Afraid to touch him, she just continued to talk. "It's me, Ariana. I heard you call to me. You called to me and I came. I'm here."

"Ariana. I'm not evil. Ah!" He shook wildly.

"I know, Nate. I know. Let your shields down, baby, so your Brethren can come get you. They'll help you get better." She couldn't stand to look at him anymore and not hold him. Taking a breath, she sat beside him and boldly encircled his body with her arms, tucking them between his back and his wings. He bucked and cried out. "Shhh. It's okay. It's okay. Let me hold you, Nate."

He eased against her body and settled his head by her heart. She caressed his cheek and ran her fingers through his hair to cradle the nape of his neck. Kissing his forehead, she closed her eyes and did her best to keep it together for his sake. "You're going to be all right, angel boy. I'll see to it." She did the only thing she could think of to soothe him. She sang him a childhood lullaby.

"Toora, loora, loora; Toora, loora, li; Toora, loora, loora; Hush, now, don't you cry." She rocked him and sang the tune over and over. His shivering body weighed heavy against her as he slowly quieted down. Breathing shallowly, she didn't care if he crushed her, as long as he returned to well-being.

"Ariana, we'll take it from here." A hand shook her shoulder gently until she opened her eyes. "I said we've got it." Looking up, she saw Raphael, Kemuel, a group of bare-chested, leather-clad angels, and Joe surrounding her and Nathanael. A couple of the angels she recognized. Others she didn't know.

"Oh. I didn't realize you'd all come already. He's in bad shape, Raphael. Please help him. Heal him. Make this addiction of his go away."

She moved to release him but he groaned and clutched onto her. "Nate, your team is here to help you. Let go, baby." But he wouldn't.

"No! You're my safe place! They can't help me. Only you. Only you!" He held on to her even tighter than before. She looked at the others, completely at a loss.

"Guys, help. He's latched on to me with a death grip."

The Brethren moved forward and amidst threats and protests, they detached him from her. His painful sobs ripped the last vestiges of her control to shreds.

"I'm so sorry, Nathanael," she sobbed. "Please forgive me and what I've done."

As the angels draped him across their arms and lifted him away, he arched back and seared her soul with his tortured stare. His hand shot out toward her. She touched her fingers to her lips, kissed them, and extended her hand, doing her best not to fall to the ground under the weight of her grief.

All but one Brethren flew off into the night. Yofi had stayed behind. He stood silent as she did her best to compose herself.

"I'll take you back to the hotel. Nothing more to be done here. Just have to wait. Link your arms around my neck, and we'll be on our way."

She wiped away the tears and put a hand on his arm. "I'm not very good at waiting, Yofi. We've got to go and get the Elixxir away from my uncle. I have to do this for Nathanael. I owe him so much."

"Don't worry. I've been keeping my senses locked on it since I located it. Come on." He grabbed her arms and wrapped them around his neck. "Here we go."

∞

Cassiel prepared for the Brethren's arrival. As he stood outside Michael and Emma's house, he watched in awe as they brought their fallen brother, twisted and contorted in their arms, to finally rest on the daybed in the study. They stood vigil while he, Raphael, and Zadkiel knelt beside him to assess how to begin their healing. The tormented angel warrior trembled and sweated profusely. At odd intervals his muscles spasmed and forced him into painful-looking angles.

"This is downright horrible," Kemuel muttered, and then raised his voice in frustration and disappointment. "I mean, we're Warrior brothers. I never suspected something like this was going on right in front of me." He shook his head and hung it low. "Why didn't he tell me he was in trouble? We could have done something for him, you know?"

"It's okay, Kemuel," Urie said, nudging him. "None of us knew. Don't beat yourself up over this. If someone wants to hide something from others, he finds ways of doing so."

"And we're here now," Cassiel said, turning away from Nathanael for a moment to help ease Kemuel's guilt. "Hopefully we can heal him up good."

Usually certain about the outcome of a healing, Cassiel chose his words carefully. He honestly didn't know how this would end. There were so many layers to cut through, as in a complicated surgery. So many intricate pathways to travel to get to the root of the problem. He knew Satan lay at the heart of it all. He'd be damned if he'd let another Brethren fall to him! Agremon had been a shining example of what happened when one fell under the influence of pure Evil. And now, with Agremon dead, he feared Nathanael's vulnerability left him open for the final conquest of his soul.

"Cassiel, Zadkiel, wave your hands right over here and tell me what you see." Raphael's brows furrowed, not a very good indicator that things would go well.

"Sure." Cassiel floated his right hand over Nathanael's forehead, seeking to scan the cerebral cortex. "Shit." Sitting back on his heels, he gave way for the third Savior to check him out. He looked at his teammates and acknowledged what each had found. Just as he figured.

"What? What's wrong, Cass?" Kemuel nudged his arm.

"We're gonna need our Great Savior Mother. Michael, can you get her now, please?" He nodded and ran out of the room. "He's all but fried. Gabriel, Urie, we need protections on him immediately, before we even proceed with the healing. He is one step away from being lost to us."

"Urie and I'll give him the highest level we've got. When Michael gets back with Emma, he can layer his supreme protection on him, as well."

"Perfect. That should hold Satan off."

"What can I do?"

Poor Kemuel. He looked like a hermit crab out of its shell. But Cassiel could understand. This wasn't new territory for him. Not too long ago, he'd lost a member of his team, Seraphiel. His surprising death hit them all hard. Now Kemuel stood to lose another so soon after getting a new recruit.

"I think you ought to go find Yofi and hook up with him. The Elixxir is still out there and must be brought back. Staying here is useless. There's nothing for you to do. It's all protections and healings. We need you out there, Kemuel. Finish the mission."

Ariana quickly changed into a pair of skinny jeans she'd managed to purchase along with the dreadfully frumpy ones, and the last clean top she had. She fixed her hair and made a private oath to succeed in retrieving the Elixxir and deliver it into Nathanael's hands. She headed out of the bathroom only to slam right into Yofi.

"Jesus! You could kill someone with that chest of yours."

"Sorry, I was about to knock on the door. We gotta go. I sense the Elixxir on the move." He traipsed over to the sliding glass door and opened it, continuing on to the balcony. She quickly followed.

"Shit. Okay, so how are we tracking it? By air, I'm assuming?"

"If you don't mind. Much quicker. Come on." He opened his arms and she wrapped hers around his neck like before. "No funny business, now. You do what I say, no question. We're dealing with satanic possession and immortality here. There's no telling what Murati is capable of doing."

"Okay. I get it."

Yofi shielded and flew them above the towering casinos of the Strip to an outlying area. Artificial day turned instantly into night. Having left Las Vegas at such a young age, she wasn't familiar with much beyond her childhood haunts. What lay beneath their flying bodies besides the blackness, she hadn't a clue.

"He's stopping. I'm bringing us lower to get a visual." She nodded. To know no one could see the two of them flying through the night sky gave her a false sense of security, as though she were impervious to any danger. "I believe its location to be around there." He pointed to an expansive mansion, heavily fortified with thick cement walls topped by barbed wire. Palm trees dotted the landscape within, along with a waterfall pool, a putting green, and a tennis court.

"He actually lives there? How can he afford the place?"

"Gabriel mentioned something to me about drug dealing."

"Well, that would explain a lot. God, I can't wait to see him go down in flames."

"Oh, he'll go down all right, Ariana. Once we have the Elixxir, there's Brethren justice to be served."

"What'll happen?"

"He'll be sent back to Hell. Murati's so far gone and has committed countless brutal crimes that he made the perfect vessel for Satan. The two will be great Hell buddies, I'm sure. Okay, let's head down, shall we?"

"Hey, Yofi, wait up!"

Ariana whipped her head around to see Kemuel fly up next to them. She closed her eyes, groaned, and leaned her forehead against Yofi's chest. *What next?*

"Hey, Kemuel. What are you doing here?"

"Nothing I can do for Nathanael at Michael's house, so I'm helping you finish his mission. Hey, Callie."

She picked her head up and mustered a smile. If he was here to help him Nathanael, she could live with that.

"Her name's Ariana."

"That's okay. He knew me in another life. Hi, Kemuel."

"Ariana, is it? You've been holding out on me."

"Yeah, well we both had our reasons for being secretive, now didn't we?"

"What do you mean?"

"Are you kidding me, Brethren Warrior? I know what you've been doing. If you'd have had a little faith in my character, you'd have known that I'd protect that secret with my life."

"I'm sorry, Cal...Ariana. You're right. Can you forgive me? Can we move on as friends? For Nathanael's sake?" His sincerity struck a chord within her, and she caved.

"For Nathanael."

"We're heading into the mansion to secure the Elixxir."

"I'm all over that, Yofi. You wanna take lead on this?"

"That's my plan, if you don't mind."

"She's all yours."

Kemuel hung back and shielded, disappearing behind her and Yofi. They made their way down to the terrace, where a vast sliding-glass door had been opened. Inside, she took a sweeping glance around at what looked like a great room and kitchen area.

"Wow. This is unreal!" Her hand involuntarily rose in awe to her lips at the crystal chandeliers and gold-embossed mirrors flanking the cavernous room. This place laughed at opulence.

"Make sure you're holding on to me at all times to stay shielded."

"Don't worry. My left hand is permanently glued to you."

"I sense the Elixxir very strongly, and it's headed this way. Kemuel, we'll play it cool, and when he takes it out of his pocket, we'll make our move."

She had no idea if Kemuel responded or not because she couldn't see or hear him. Being human had its limitations. He could have been right in front of her face and she wouldn't have known. Unsettling for her, but she realized what a great stealth tool it made in times such as these.

Murati sauntered into the great room and over to the bar. He poured himself a double shot of scotch over ice. Picking up a remote that sat on the counter, he pushed a button and flames came to life in a fireplace that took up a wall of its own. She watched with curiosity as he traversed the mantle of photographs, stopping for a few moments in front of two in particular. He took a long sip of scotch and formed his right hand into a gun while pointing it at the pictures. He laughed and raised his glass.

Who's in those photos?

"Here's to you, dear old friend. May you and your family rot in Hell for all the years of crap you put me through. If we ever meet up in another life, I'll make sure to enjoy killing you all over again. But wait, we won't. I forgot, I'm immortal now and you're good and dead! Ha ha!" He slapped his hand to his thigh and continued laughing all the way to the opening onto the terrace.

Ariana pulled Yofi over to get a look at the photos. One was of her parents, and another of just her. *Son-of-a-bitch psycho!* Her heart pounded out of her chest and her hands clenched into fists.

"Easy there, girl. Easy. You're gonna tear my shirt. I'm assuming these are your parents and you?"

"Yes." She loosened her grip and took a deep breath. "And if there's a way to kill the bastard, I'm gonna see to it he dies a slow and painful death. Right after he gets to know some lovely men in Cell Block C. If you know what I mean."

"Come on. Let's see what he does next."

Only a few moments passed before Murati moved to a chaise longue and set his glass down on a mosaic table beside it. He reached into his breast pocket, brought out a small brass box, and began fiddling with the closure.

"This is it, Kemuel. Be ready to pounce."

"Hey! You got a human attached to you." She tugged on Yofi's sleeve. "What do you expect me to do? Hold on while you wrestle the box away from him? This isn't gonna work."

"Damn, I hadn't thought about that. Freakin' rookie mistake. You're right. Okay, let me think. All right, as we move in, let go of me and run like hell to find cover. I'll pick you up when we're through. Shit, he's taking something out. Go!"

She let go of her lifeline and watched the new Brethren fade to invisible before her eyes. She quickly spotted a circular retaining wall with a raised bed of plants and made a run for it. She dared not look over at her uncle. As much as she wanted to see him die, as much as she put up a brave front, she feared him and couldn't chance being frozen in place should their eyes meet. Only a couple more steps and she'd be covered.

Suddenly, a tether surrounded her mid-section and stopped her in her tracks. Reaching down with both hands, she feverishly fought to escape its unshakable grasp. It yanked her back a few steps, and when she yelped and turned around to see what had gotten hold of her, she saw something she knew had not come from the mortal world. *I'm in deep shit.*

A reddish radiance surrounded her waist and trailed across

the back yard straight to her Uncle Eddie's right hand. Above him, dangling in the air by another red, glowing lasso, were Yofi and Kemuel, arms and wings secured to their bodies. He made twisting gestures with his left hand and the angels grimaced. She didn't know how he'd bested them when they'd gone in shielded, but there was no denying he had the advantage at the moment. Without thinking, she pulled on the strangely lit rope around her.

"Hey! Leave them alone, you son-of-a-bitch!"

Murati turned with fire in his eyes and Evil in his grin. He raised his left hand higher and tightened it slowly into a fist. The two Brethren spun around and she could hear them groaning.

Her heart broke at their painful grunts. "I said leave them alone! It's me you want. Let them go and you can have me."

"Oh, our meeting is long overdue, and I will have you all right, my dear. But I'm not releasing these two. Seems everyone around here wants something, and the only one going to get anything is me. Ha! I win!"

He tossed his left hand about wildly, which in turn further wrapped and trapped the angels within the supernatural binding's choking grip. He then guided the hulking package over to the fire pit, where with a pointed glare, he started a bonfire.

"Lovely day for a pig roast, don't you think?" He looked over at her and winked as he rotated them over the ever-increasing flames.

"No! Uncle Eddie, no!" She strained against her bindings, unable to endure the scene unfolding before her. "Don't do this! Please, I'll do anything you want, just don't hurt them. Let them go."

"Anything? Now that does sound intriguing. What could I want from you that could be more attractive than serving up some angels for a snack? Oh, I know." He cut the cord between him and the evil lariats, yet they remained firmly noosed around his captives. "I want you to drink this." He stalked up to her and presented the Elixxir flask to her.

"No! Ariana, don't do it!"

She couldn't believe what he'd just said. He wanted her to drink the Elixxir of Life, like he had. But why? "I don't understand. The bottle alone has brought me nothing but pain and misery. Why would you share the contents of it with me?"

"Ah, yes. Your parents' deaths. An unfortunate by-product of the dangers associated with our business, I'm afraid."

"That's all they were to you?" Tears smarted at the corners of her eyes. "An unfortunate by-product? What's happened to you, Uncle Eddie? Where's the man I idolized as a child? Where's the man who sat for hours with me, describing the far-away places those curious objects represented? Where is the man, period?"

"I'm right here." He opened his arms wide, preening like a peacock. "I'm the improved model. Eternity is a long time to live. I should like you as a companion to join me. I need someone who has been connected to the Elixxir as long as I have, and who would appreciate what it offers to those who possess it."

"You're a monster," she seethed. "How could you kill my parents and destroy my life? How? And now you want me to go through eternity with you as your companion?" She shook her head in amazement and revulsion. "Well, I don't buy your line for one minute. What's your angle? What are you really after?"

"I'm after vengeance and glory!" Flames shot higher into the air, threatening to set the Brethren's wings afire. "I was to have the Elixxir when your father brought it back. It was my money he used to acquire it. Mine. Your father had been looking for a big score. But he had no capital. He had everything tied up in real estate. So he came to me one day with this hot prospect but no money to see it through. I fronted him the money and he came back with the Elixxir and hid it. From me! Of all people. He deserved his vicious end, just like your mother did. Always taunting me about playing second fiddle to your father and flaunting her body at me like such a tease but never following through."

While he ranted, she stood reeling. Being so young at the time, she was never privy to her parents' business dealings, but had always thought her father a fair businessman. Now, to hear this inflammatory recounting of what had happened twenty years ago made her ill. She didn't know what to accept as truth, and it didn't matter at this point. Here she stood, prisoner of a madman, while the Brethren were being roasted on a spit. She had to do something. His increasingly crazed voice burst through her musings.

"And so, you're right. I have an ulterior motive here. You will drink this and spend the rest of eternity shackled like a slave at my side, witnessing how I take over the world! Yes, watching and incurring my wrath, day after day, as I think of new ways to humiliate and torture you with no one left in your life to care."

She couldn't fathom the idea of eternity or the true implications of what he suggested, but she did see two angels in need of rescuing, and made the only decision that she believed would end the current predicament they were in. "Okay, I'll drink it. But if you don't follow through with your end of the bargain and free those two, I will spend the rest of our eternity making it a living hell for *you*."

"Ariana! You don't know what you're saying. Forget about us. We'll be fine." Kemuel's voice shook with a ferocity she'd never heard in him before.

"I promise to free them once you've taken from the flask." He uncorked the bottle and touched the lip of it to hers, tipping it forward so her head had to lean back. "That's my girl. Drink! Only a drop."

"No!"

A scent of citrus hit her nose, but when a drop of the Elixxir fell to her tongue, a bitter taste took over, as though she'd been chewing orange rind mixed with coffee. She gagged but recovered, not wanting to give him an ounce of satisfaction.

A strange sensation washed across her body. From her head all the way down to her toes, she could sense each cell splitting, neurons firing, and making new connections. And then, as quickly as it came, it went away. She frowned.

That's it? Am I immortal now? Can I break free?

She tried, wriggling around, but the bindings were secure.

"Only a drop for now, my dear. We must take it slowly. Two drops and your transformation will be complete."

"Release them." She tossed her head to indicate the angels.

He whipped out another lasso and wrapped it tightly around her throat. "Brethren, you're free. One move toward us, however, and she will suffer greatly. Be on your way. You'll get nothing from me. Tell your illustrious boss Satan has won today!"

The luminous ribbons that were so tightly wound around the two angels faded and disappeared. Before they could fall into the fiery pit, their wings lifted them up and away. But they didn't move.

"We'll not leave her here, Murati." Hovering in the air, Kemuel turned to her. "We will not leave you!"

"You have no choice. Come closer and she dies a slow, painful death. The one drop is barely enough to add a couple hundred years to her life. I should very much like to suffocate her slowly across those many days."

"Kemuel, go. Take Yofi, and get out of here." He flew toward her, pain and guilt etching lines in his face. Suddenly, she couldn't breathe. A vise cinched about her neck. As she struggled in vain to free herself, she mouthed, "Please."

Kemuel backed off. She coughed madly as Murati loosened the cord.

"You must be a bit thick in the head, angel. In a few moments she would have become most uncomfortable since there would have been no more air to breathe. Go now."

"Ariana, we will come back for you. I promise." She nodded, gasping for much-needed air. Kemuel pointed at the possessed man. "Mark my words, Old Man Forever, we will be back, and if you so much as harm a hair on her head, you will meet with the full fury of the Brethren."

Eddie, in turn, chuckled. Then his laughter grew into an unearthly cackle and he shook his head.

Kemuel floated to Yofi and tapped him on the arm. As they flew off, she wondered if she'd ever really see them again. Uncle Eddie wouldn't keep her alive for long. She'd wised up over the years. There were no plans to make her truly immortal, only to make her suffer.

Well, at the very least, I've saved two angels. Maybe I'll see them on my way up to heaven.

Chapter Sixteen

"*I* sense Evil nearby. The Evil-doers must be vanquished! Let me take them down. Every last one of them." Nathanael writhed on the bed and fought unsuccessfully against the Brethren shackles binding his hands and feet. Chills wracked his body and his reddish Warrior aura flickered about him. He looked at Emma and Michael standing beside him, and struggled to understand why his team had restrained him. "Why have you done this to me? You've turned your backs on me, on our mission. You've betrayed the contract. Let me go and we'll take care of business like before. I'll forgive you and forget this ever happened."

He held out his bound wrists, fully expecting compliance. He offered them to Emma, and she shook her head. He moved on to Michael, who stepped back. He roared his displeasure as his eyes burned and slammed his clenched fists against the sheets.

"No, don't listen to me! The evil is inside me. It's in all of us. You must kill me, now! Ahh!"

Beads of sweat trickled down his temples, leaving angry, red trails behind them. He couldn't take the war on his soul much longer. Stabbing pains like hot pokers shot through both sides of his brain and heart. Satan wanted acceptance of the Evil he'd planted inside him, or his death, and it was driving him mad in the process.

"Ariana, help me. I need you." Tears blurred his vision as he sought her out. But she was nowhere to be seen. "Where is she? Where's Ariana?" He rocked back and forth, sobbing and muttering over and over again, "Where's my safe place? I need my safe place. Ariana...."

Emma's voice drizzled into his brain like honey. "Brethren, let's get to work."

∞

"He hasn't said anything since the last healing session, Emma. Is that a good sign or a bad one?"

"Don't know yet, Urie. The Saviors have done all we can to help him. But as with any addict, he must meet us halfway."

"You bring people back from near death and they go on to live out the rest of their days just fine. Why should he be any different?"

"Because an addict like me is never truly healed. Isn't that right, Raphael?" Nathanael wriggled on the bed he'd been laid upon and glanced around. He didn't remember being taken to Michael's house.

"The angel arises and speaks!"

"And the angel hears, as well, Cass." He raised his fists. "Now take these damned things off me."

Michael stepped forward and released him from all of his bindings. "They were for your safety as much as for ours."

Although there were no marks, he instinctively rubbed his wrists. "I've heard every last word you all had to say since you tore me away from Ariana. I'm damaged goods. I can't be trusted anymore to fulfill my Brethren duties without going on a rampage. Don't suppose you have a plan for my replacement."

"What are you talking about? We never said we didn't trust you. We're concerned about your ability to do your job safely. And who's suggesting E.L. replace you? You may need to be reassigned while you go through the steps of recovery. But we would never replace you. Michael has purged Satan's threaded connection to you, so there is no threat of you succumbing to Evil any longer. We healed you to a point. But it's gonna be a daily battle for you to control your endorphin rushes once you're back on Warrior duty."

"Couldn't Satan get ahold of me again, though, Raph?"

"Anything's possible, but it's up to you to keep him away. Now, Michael will give you a talisman to help you through these first days and weeks of detox, but we're gonna want to wean you off of it. You don't want to become so reliant on it that you forget how to use your own innate powers to fight off Evil."

"Right. It's gonna be a long freakin' road back from Hell. Satan's been working on me for a long time now."

"That's why you have me." Joe stepped around the goliaths in the room and sat on the bed next to him.

"Joe!" He shook his head. "Man, I fucked up big tonight."

"Tomorrow's another day, dude. I'm here for you."

"Thanks, man." Maybe Joe could get him through this. With Ariana by his side, he knew he could do it. "So, where's Ariana? I need to see her."

The Brethren passed cryptic glances between them. He remembered the stern looks they'd given her as they took him away. Before he had a chance to question them further, Yofi and Kemuel burst into the room.

"We got a situation. Everyone needs to mobilize fast."

"What's going on, Kem?"

"Murati's got her."

"And the Elixxir," Yofi chimed in.

Nathanael jumped from the bed and got up in Kemuel's face, rage instantly hitting him hard. "What the hell are you talking about? And you left her with him? What were you thinking?"

"Whoa, back off, man." Michael and Urie grabbed him by his arms and provided a protective wall for Kemuel. "Murati's got Satan in him and he blocked our ability to communicate. He's got mad powers, more than we've seen in a long time. We were roped and trussed in this demonized lasso, and then hung over flames to be roasted like pigs. She begged him to let us go and made a deal with him. He's got her. Made her drink some of the Elixxir. We tried to contact you but couldn't until we were on Michael's property. He doesn't have anything pleasant planned for her."

"Shit. He wants her good and dead, Kemuel. That's his plan." He looked at the men flanking him. "Let go of me, now. Kemuel, take us to where he's holding her."

"You should stay here," Cassiel said. "We'll go. This is exactly the kind of scenario you need to stay away from right now."

"Are you fucking kidding me? That woman is the only thing that's kept me sane! There's no way you're keeping me from going after her."

"Isn't she the one who set you off in the first place?"

He turned on him, fuming. "Shut the hell up, Urie. I'd been skirting the edge for hours before I left. She was just a convenient excuse. I understood why she did what she did. I let the anger feed the darkness inside me and take control. Now, who do I have to knock out to let me go?"

No one said a word. "All right, then let's move out."

୧

Relief mixed with dread as Ariana watched the horizon after the Brethren had gone. How soon could they return with reinforcements? Would they return at all, or cut their losses and wait for another chance to get the Elixxir? And how was Nathanael doing? She missed him so much. He'd been the only one who truly knew her and all the secrets and nightmares she'd lived with, and still he stood by her. Having him torn away from her like that had been a kick to the gut and squeezed her heart so much it literally hurt. The Brethren blamed her for his condition. She could see it in their eyes. And they were right to. Her impulsiveness and lies had screwed up everything and pushed him over the edge.

"So much pain and sorrow in those eyes," Murati said

wistfully as he played with a stray lock of her hair. "Good." He tossed the strands in her face and turned away.

"Are you going to keep me tied up and standing out here indefinitely?"

"Haven't decided." He picked up his glass of scotch, swished it around, and took a sip. "Although I should bring you inside. The neighbors might talk. Oh wait, I have no neighbors. Not for miles. You can stand out here and rot for all I care."

"Can you please take the rope from around my throat at least?"

He sighed and strolled back over to her, waved his hand, and it disappeared. But then, he grasped her neck with both hands and fiery orbs glared right back at her. "Do you know how easy it would be to kill you right now? Just one quick twist and snap ought to do it. But where's the fun in that? It'd be over too soon and then you'd be alive again in minutes. Twenty years I've searched for you, to kill you. And now that the time is upon us, I find myself awash with emotion and at a loss as to what to do with you."

"Well, that's a good sign. Maybe you want to spare me and forget the whole killing-me plan."

"No, I'm gonna kill you, all right, when your hundred years is up. But I'm thinking torture might be in order first. Yes, that would take a good long while and I should get much pleasure drawing out the pain. Should I go with breaking bones, or lashings?"

She shook her head, refusing to show him the abject terror he'd instilled within her. "You are one very sick man," she muttered.

"You'd do well not to piss me off, woman!"

Ariana's heart flipped and leapt to her throat. No, pissing him off was not what she'd intended. He wielded two glowing strands and wrapped them around her wrists. He secured each end to a palm tree on either side of her and pulled them taut.

"Ahh!" Her muscles strained, stretched nearly beyond their capability.

"Shut your trap!" He waved his hand over her face and her voice went silent. "That's better. Now, today's punishment shall begin. Would you like to know what it will be? Of course you would. That lashing idea sounds perfect. One for every year you stole from me. That would be twenty. But don't worry. It'll only hurt for a little while. Since you're not fully immortal yet, I'm not quite sure how long the pain will last. But the best part about this is I can do it to you all over again tomorrow because I'm sure by then you'll be good as new! Ha!"

He snapped his fingers as he strutted around her, and an orange flame of a whip extended from his palm. She closed her eyes and prayed she could handle his abuse. He grunted and she heard a sharp crack from behind her. Sudden, intense pain traveled down the right side of her back. She tensed and opened her mouth to scream, but nothing came out. Another lash from the whip, this time down her spine, sent her knees buckling and tears spilled onto her cheeks. Her skin burned as raw nerve endings smarted from exposure to the air.

A third strike hit her lower back and curled around her waist. She hung limply from her tethered wrists. Delirium settled in, and she faded in and out of awareness. Unconsciousness couldn't come soon enough for her. Even death would have been welcome.

What have I done to deserve such a fucked-up life? Whatever have I done?

The fourth blow left her without an answer but sent her into blissful darkness. She had no sense of time, but Uncle Eddie called out each strike of the lash. As she lapsed in and out of consciousness she heard ten and then fifteen.

Where is the blessed twentieth?

ଔ

Yelling.

She heard voices yelling and a crackling like electrical charges all around her. Opening her eyes, she marveled at the sight. There were winged Brethren flying all about, glowing and wielding swords against a sea of lightning bolts emanating from Eddie's palms. Brilliant flashes of energy charged the air around her, raising the tiny hairs on her skin. Hundreds of craggy ribbons lunged toward each angel, making for a dangerous and frenetic scene. Dozens of after-images burned their marks before her until she could barely see.

Hopes rose and fell at once. They'd come back! But how could they possibly fight and win against such a powerful monster? At the moment, it didn't look good at all. A quick flick of Eddie's wrist and another lash-strike landed hard on her shoulders. The sound of wailing surprised her. He'd given her voice back.

"Listen, Brethren! Hear the lilting music of torture only I can deliver!"

The whipping increased in intensity and frequency. Knowing her voice had returned, she refused to utter another sound and feed into his sadistic plan. She might not be in control of the situation, but she sure as hell was in charge of her reactions. Skin on fire, she could actually feel blood trickling down her back from open wounds. One distinct voice amongst the many broke through her agony and touched her heart. *Nathanael.*

"Tonight, Murati, you die!"

He roared and descended to the ground. Taking one ominous-looking step after another toward her, his sword blocked and batted away the incessant barrage of destructive energy focused directly on him.

"Hold on, Red," he shouted. "I'm coming for you, as I promised. Brethren! Swords together!"

As they changed formation and brought their swords up, all the bolts blended into one, and the wall of metal reflected the massive energy, sending sparks shooting high into the sky and back at Murati's palms.

"Ahh!" Satan's lackey buckled under the strain and dropped to his knees.

The lightning show ended, the lashings stopped, and her

bindings faded away. She crumpled to the ground, but in spite of the pain managed to crawl to a relatively safe area by a raised flower bed, where she watched in horror as her uncle transformed right before her eyes.

Buttons popped, fabric ripped under the strain, and then, along with an ungodly scream, the very skin itself tore away as a grotesque creature emerged. An oily black sheen coated his scaly body. Howling, he stretched to his full height, dwarfing all of the Brethren present. Two red, curling horns protruded and elongated from his temples, and his clawed hands fisted in the air as though announcing he had arrived—whatever the hell he was.

"Brethren, be warned! Your existence is meaningless, and I shall take pleasure in meting out your death! I am Abaddon. Look into my eyes and you shall see your end!"

Unable to take in the unfolding scene any longer, she shrieked and backed up even farther, but as she did so, something glinted from the ground by what used to be her uncle's body. *The Elixxir!* She had to get to it somehow and keep it secure.

The Brethren were up to their eyeballs in scary shit and she needed to pitch in, terror be damned. She monitored the situation for a few moments and saw the demon's attention rested fully on the angels. Seeing her chance, she scrambled over to grab the flask, and found herself looking right into the eyes of what nightmares were made of.

Evil took all shapes and forms, but in the millennia of fighting and warring, none had ever materialized such as the one that now stood before the Brethren Warrior. He wouldn't have the chance to deal out justice to Murati like he'd wanted; but then, Evil had taken care of that for him. So he would take care of the Evil that stood before them now. The familiar endorphin rush had coursed through his veins like a spark in dry brush as he'd flown over to save Ariana. With Michael's talisman around his neck, no darkness could penetrate his soul, so he now gave free rein to the fire, the rage, and his desire for justice.

The coordinated efforts of all Brethren would be necessary here. He knew that. Understood the protocols. But when he saw her, battered and bleeding as she scrambled out of her hiding spot and retrieved the Elixxir, all reason left him. She'd caught Abaddon's attention and now stared, terror-stricken, into the demon's eyes.

"Michael, protection! Now! Ariana's got the Elixxir!"

Michael extended his left hand toward her, but his attempts to protect her were flicked away like a gnat by this demon from Hell.

"Shit, Gabriel! Urie! Help him!"

All the Protectors combined their energies to wrap a protective dome around her and the Elixxir. The demon trudged right through it. The Warriors laid in their attack with jabs and slices to his scaly skin, but the wounds instantly healed, just as their own skin did. All efforts were ignored.

"Ariana! Toss me the Elixxir. It's what he wants." But she remained frozen in her place. "Toss it!"

No response, and Abaddon closed in on her.

The entire team raised their swords and flew over to defend her, but couldn't get close enough. The behemoth batted them away as if they were toy action figures.

"The Elixxir will be mine, mortal." His razor-sharp claws loomed ever closer to her and he plucked her right from where she'd been sitting like a stone figure.

He lifted her high in the air and she came to life, wriggling and protesting, hurling curses.

"You will never have it!" She opened the flask and poured the liquid down her throat. Coughing and gagging, she lost control and her hands let go of the flask. Nathanael looked on in horror as a greenish glow formed around her and beams of light shot out of her eyes. Her body shook like a tree being uprooted in the midst of a tornado. An inhuman screech threatened to deafen them all.

Abaddon was not a happy demon.

Normalcy seemed to return to Ariana as the light show receded, but as it did so, she stretched her arms out wide, grabbed hold of each horn, and pulled his face down to meet hers. "You've met your match, demon!"

Pulling those horns down even farther and twisting with the power of a legion of immortals, she wrestled the demon to the ground and stuck the tips into the earth. Nathanael looked on in amazement and pride at his woman, now an immortal with more strength then that of all the Brethren put together. "Warriors! Come deliver your Brethren justice!" She stood before them, a warrior in her own right.

Pulled from his stupor, Nathanael charged straight in like a bull, with Kemuel and Yofi joining him on both sides. Kemuel stuck Abaddon through the chest, deep into the earth, while Yofi skewered his gut on his blade. Nathanael severed his legs and arms and raised his sword to deliver the final blow. The inscription on the blade blazed. His eyes glazed over, ready for the execution, but he caught sight of Ariana and stopped. He wanted to do it. His body thrummed with the need for the kill. But would he cross a line he could never cross back over again?

"Do it, Nate. I'm here. I'll bring you back. Look to me for your safe place."

He nodded, and with the force of ten warriors, swung his sword. Light splayed out from Abaddon's neck and he ceased to exist. The sword absorbed the demon's blood in a brilliant display. Nathanael shuddered, closed his eyes, and fell to his knees, groaning. Sticking the blade into the ground before him, he anticipated the pain and hunger for more.

Look to me, Nathanael, for your safe place.

She had spoken to him in his mind and he took a shaky breath. Hanging his head, he extended a trembling hand. A warm, soft hand closed around his. He grabbed her to him in a fierce embrace and drank in her unique essence, something he hadn't noticed about her before. It damn near intoxicated him, and he smiled for the first time since...he didn't know when. He nuzzled her hair and then held her from him, leaning his forehead against hers.

"My God, Ariana, you crazy fool!" He raked his hands through her hair to cradle her head and placed a crushing kiss on her lips. He tasted the salt of tears, not knowing whether they had been his or hers. "I almost lost you! Do you realize what that would have done to me? Whatever possessed you to drink the Elixxir?"

"Nothing was working, Nate. The Brethren were completely outmatched by that...that thing." She caressed his cheeks and shook her head. "I don't know. I guess I thought that maybe with the power of the Elixxir I could help in some small way. There seemed nothing left to do. And...I couldn't bear losing you. You need me too much. And, hell, I need you more."

Chapter Seventeen

$\mathcal{N}$athanael brought Ariana back to Emma and Michael's house. Emma greeted them in the foyer.

"Nathanael."

He nodded. "Emma, good to see you."

"Good to see you, too. You have a healing session with me after you debrief with the boys, and Ariana, I'd like to meet with you now. You're not the only one here who's been transformed from mortal to immortal. We've taken different paths but it all ends at the same point, immortality. I think we should take advantage of the gathering in there, don't you?"

"I guess so. I've got questions. Lots of questions."

"And I'm sure the Brethren would like to know how your newfound immortality has manifested within you. What, if any, special powers you may have acquired. So, you, head on into the study there. The boys are already debriefing. Ariana, follow me, please."

He leaned down and kissed her lightly on the lips, cupped her cheek, and smiled. "Hey, I'll see you soon, Red. Be good and play nice."

"You, too. Stay cool, calm. If things get dicey in there, think of me." She ruffled his hair and followed Emma down the hall.

Nathanael entered the study, or lion's den, since it sounded like a lot of snarling and arguing going on. He took a deep breath and joined the fray.

"What's all the shouting about?"

Kemuel spoke up first. "What the hell happened back there? That's what all the shouting is about. How the hell did things go so wrong? Why?"

"E.L. is fucking around with us again. He did it before, with Emma and me, remember? And he did it again today with all of us."

"There's got to be a way to circumvent his ability to screw with us, Michael. How can we do our jobs here if our powers can be dampened or made null and void at his will?"

"Kemuel, he's always got a plan. You know that. We do what we think we should do in a given situation. If he has other designs, well, he lets us know by limiting our capabilities."

"I get it, but what I have a problem with is that he made us *all* ineffective. None of us could do anything to that demon until Ariana drank the Elixxir and turned immortal on us. Speaking of which, we were supposed to deliver it back to the Beyond. What are we gonna do now? Deliver an empty flask?"

Nathanael sat on the floor by the fireplace. "Good question. I wonder what E.L. will have us do. I'm sure he'll weigh in any time now. Technically, it no longer exists."

"Technically, it exists inside Ariana." Gabriel tapped a finger to his chin. "What will he have us do about that? Speaking of the enigma himself, he's buzzing me right now." He took out his cell phone and answered the call. "Sir? Yes, sir." He put his phone away.

"That's it?" Michael shook his head. "Three words and two of them were the same."

"Well, we have one of our questions answered. You're to escort Ariana Kupi to the Beyond. You have twenty-four hours to get her there."

"Wow." Cassiel whacked him on the arm. "Nice of him to give you a chance to recuperate a bit."

"Is he for real? I'm beginning to question our fearless

leader's sanity. What the hell good does it do to bring her there besides freak her out?"

"I don't know, but you gotta do it. Twenty-four hours."

Nathanael threw back his chair upon standing and stalked out of the meeting. He needed some space and time to think.

ଔ

Ariana's head buzzed. Ultra-sharp, brilliant colors flooded her vision to the point of pain. She could hear her heartbeat, and noticed it had slowed considerably. Blood cells shushed through her veins and arteries, and the sensation of tiny worms crawling under her skin rattled her. She hadn't felt this way earlier. Maybe she'd been too keyed up to notice. Now, with each step she took toward the bedroom, she wanted to chop her head off more and more: a high-pitched incessant ring had begun, and showed no signs of stopping.

"Hey, Emma, do you have any aspirin or something stronger? My head is exploding, and it's like I've been infested by creepy crawlies. I can't take it anymore."

"We don't need aspirin around here, so I'm sorry, I don't. But let's get you settled in here and I'll check you out. Okay?"

"Yeah, sure, fine." She lay down on the bed.

Emma closed her eyes and rubbed her hands together. When she opened them, she put one hand on Ariana's forehead and one on her heart. Emma grunted, furrowing her brows. Her breaths came in shallow huffs. When she removed her hands, her composure returned.

"What the hell's wrong with me?" Ariana slowly sat up on the bed.

"You drank the Elixxir?"

"Yes."

"How much?"

"Whatever was left in the flask."

Emma sighed and rubbed her temples. "This isn't good, I gotta tell you the truth. Not good at all."

"Great. Am I gonna turn into one of those grotesque demons, like my uncle did, or something horrible like that?"

"No, nothing like that." She shook her head and patted her arm. "And from what I've been told, your uncle's soul was taken over by Satan, who craves power of any kind. The problem lies with the fact that the Elixxir is not meant for human consumption. It's for immortals whose host bodies have incurred an injury that cannot be healed through human medicine or by a Savior's hand. It's long since been lost to us, until now. Since you've ingested it, along with gaining immortal powers, it's behaving like an allergen or toxin in your system. I'm concerned that in a worst-case scenario, it could kill you."

"Well then, how the hell do we get it out of me?"

"Good question. I don't know. But what I think I can do is slow down your body's reaction to it so that you can manage until we figure something out. Lie down again, and I'll see what I can do."

Emma rubbed her hands together and began a slow progression of touches and hovering of her hands over Ariana's entire body, from her toes to her head. Once finished, she had to admit to feeling somewhat better. The ringing had faded and she couldn't hear her inner workings as loudly as before. The crawling worm sensation provided only a faint distraction.

"Wow. You're good. Thank you." She sat up and hugged her. "I hope we can figure out what to do about me permanently, though. I'm not ready to die just yet. I'll put up a helluva fight."

"I would expect nothing less from Serena's best friend." She offered her a warm smile.

"You know, I'm concerned about Nathanael. I'd like to go see him."

"Well, we're all done here for now, so let's go have a look."

She put her arm around her shoulder and squeezed as she shepherded Ariana out of the bedroom. They entered the study together and all Brethren conversation ceased as one by one they stared at her. She took a deep breath and stared right back at them. Never one to let anything stew, she broke the silence.

"Listen guys, I know you don't like me much. I know you blame me for Nathanael going off the deep end. But let me say that—"

"We don't blame you. We actually would like to thank you." Gabriel approached her and extended a hand. Her jaw dropped at the unexpected gratitude. "It's customary to shake hands when one is extended."

"Oh, right! Yes, well, you're welcome, I guess?" She shook his hand.

"We thank you for saving Kemuel's and Yofi's lives earlier today. We haven't seen such selflessness in a human in centuries. Some of us, not at all. So consider yourself an honorary member of the crew."

"Oh, I'm no angel. I mean, uh, ha. Well." Caught completely off guard, she shook her head and laughed. "Aw, hell. I appreciate the honor. So where is he?" She looked around the room, frowning, and then back at Gabriel.

"He stepped out for a few minutes."

"What's wrong? I know something's wrong. I can see it in your faces. It wasn't only blame I thought I saw when we came in. It was pity. What gives?"

"Our boss called. He wants to see you."

"Oh, is that all?" She laughed. "No biggie. I'm a charmer. He may be angry with me for drinking the Elixxir, but when I walk out of his office we'll be making plans for a family dinner together."

The Brethren exchanged dubious looks.

"Oh, come on! What can be so bad?"

"It's not so much the 'who' you're going to see, as the 'where'...along with the 'who'."

"All right, Gabriel, you're making me dizzy here. I'm going to go look for Nathanael and find out what's really going on."

She turned to leave the study and stormed out the front door. "Nathanael! Where are you?"

"Over here, by the swings."

She raced to the side of the house where a child's swing set stood dwarfed by the mammoth angel leaning against it. "Hey, how are ya?"

"Just dandy. More importantly, how are you?" He offered her his hand. She took it.

"I'm fine, for now. Emma shared some scary stuff with me that I don't even want to think about right now. So, stop deflecting, and tell me what's bothering you. Does it have anything to do with this trip I gotta take to your boss?"

"It has everything to do with it." He grabbed her to him and held on as though he'd fall through the earth without her there to anchor him. She rubbed his back and leaned into the embrace.

"Why? Tell me. If I know, I can work through it, but ignorance will only make me very afraid."

"I have to bring you to the Beyond within twenty-four hours. E.L wants to see you."

"Okay, so where is this Beyond place? Should we be going now? Is it far from here?"

"Nope. It'll only take a few minutes to get there."

"Uh huh. And are we taking your bike or do we need to borrow someone's car?"

"No, we don't need the bike or a car."

She shrugged away from his warmth and glared. "Nate, enough already. I'm through with playing twenty questions and you don't usually beat around the bush."

"The Beyond is where we, the Brethren, come from. It's not a place for mortals. I know you drank the Elixxir and you're nearly immortal now, but you are still very much a human in most ways. I'm concerned that going there could prove to be too much for you."

"And? What's the worst that can happen?"

"I don't know. No one knows. That's the problem. No one but Brethren and other angels have been there."

She stepped back into his arms. "Oh, Nate. If you want, I'll wear sunglasses, or you can blindfold me if you think it will be too much for me to take in."

"This isn't funny, Red."

"Nothing has been funny for a while. Let's go already and get this over with. Maybe your boss can help me get this stuff out of me. Apparently, I'm not meant to ingest the Elixxir, and I'm having an allergic reaction to it. It's becoming toxic in my body." She looked up at him. "At least that's what Emma thinks."

"Shit." He kissed her forehead and let his lips linger, then worked his way to her temple. "Are you in any pain?"

"No, only a nagging headache on the fringe and a vague crawling sensation under my skin."

He caressed her cheeks with the backs of his hands. His eyes spoke of fear and desire as he lowered his lips to plunder hers, searing their souls together. The urgency brought tears to her eyes and caused her breath to hitch. She wrapped her arms around his waist and held on for dear life, not wanting the magic to end, not wanting to meet the next inevitable moment. But being a realist, she knew what had to be done. Tearing herself away from him, she steadied herself by holding on to his arms and looked up at his beautiful, hardened face pinched with dread.

"As much as I would like to take you to a room right now and have my dirty little way with you, I think we need to go. We need to do this first. Why delay? Huh?"

He closed his eyes, as though he could shut out the world. When he looked back at her, a new resolve appeared. "You're right. The sooner we get this over with, the better. I just don't have a clue how E.L. is going to deal with you. That makes me nervous. But I promise I won't leave your side."

"That makes everything a whole lot better. Come on, let's say our goodbyes and head out to Neverland."

∞

Returning to Nathanael's apartment in Sedona afforded the two the privacy needed for their journey to the Beyond. Having flown all the way from Las Vegas in his arms, she proclaimed herself a veteran angel flyer and didn't mind the few minutes it would take to get home. While she showered, he popped her clothes into the wash for a quick refresh. They swapped places and she fought to keep her nerves from taking over while waiting for them to dry.

She sat down to read. Motorcycle magazines weren't cutting it, but his library of books proved fascinating. True crimes, mysteries, and suspense novels lined his bookshelves from top to bottom. Nope, a novel wouldn't take her mind off the impending meeting, either. She wandered over to his desk littered with files upon files of bounty cases. Some were stamped with a huge red "Closed" on them. Just as her finger slid under the opening of one of the files, the buzzer for the dryer went off. She cut her finger on the edge, winced, and watched in amazement as it healed right before her eyes. Would she ever get used to that? Would she have to?

Her clothes smelled rain-fresh as she pulled them from the dryer. The scent coaxed a smile from her lips. She dropped the towel and bent over to step into her panties. Warm, soft hands suddenly rested just above the cleft of her butt and lightly massaged up her back. They were followed by seductive, feather-light kisses along her spine. Her eyes instinctively closed, and her head spun from the tender touches. She straightened up and turned into the waiting arms of a gloriously naked angel.

"We shouldn't." She sighed, betraying her own words by adjusting so every possible inch of her body touched his.

"Yes, yes we should." His voice and manhood had thickened with desire, while strong hands caressed her shoulders and back. "I've rethought this hasty trip, and decided that without knowing what will happen, this is very much called for right now. I need you, Ariana, forever by my side. If it happens I can't have that, at least I can have now." Wings came from around his back, encircling her and teasing her already sensitized skin.

He needs me. But is he in love with me? If I live through this, can his need be enough for me? It will have to be, because for the love of God, I'm in love with him, and can't live without him by my side.

She peered up at him through misty eyes and spoke despite the lumps in her throat. "Then let's make now last forever. Kiss me. Touch me. Make love to me, angel of mine."

He tightened his wings about her and gentled a kiss upon her lips that transformed into an all- out assault, removing all thought. Hoisting her onto the washing machine, he spread his wings and her legs, and touched her. And she him.

His skin vibrated beneath her fingers, and his aura cast a reddish glow about the small laundry room. As he entered her inch by painstaking inch, he sucked in a breath and she moaned, delirious with the sense of completeness their coming together always gave her. Keeping inside her, Nathanael brought them to his bedroom, where a king-size, raised bed stood centered against the far wall.

"Oh, my...." she murmured, staring wide-eyed.

"What's wrong?"

"I think I might get lost on that monstrosity!" She gave him a worried look at first and then burst out laughing.

"Ooh, don't stop laughing. You feel so good."

He laid her upon the bed and tickled her ribs. She giggled and tickled him back. They rolled and tussled across the great expanse of bed until abruptly, he stopped them, becoming quite serious with his piercing gaze. Not uttering a word, he began a slow, torturous rhythm that she quickly met with a pulse of her own. As the fire in her belly grew, she quickened their pace and stroked his wings until they were both shouting and grabbing at each other. Sweat collected between her breasts, and he bent down to lick and tease each peak until she could stand it no longer and climaxed, with him following right behind. Tucking his wings away, he collapsed beside her with a groan and collected her into his arms. She could have sworn she heard him whisper, "Mine."

She closed her eyes and reveled in his latent power. It amazed her how at ease she became with him surrounding her completely, as though his very presence wiped away all the horrors from her past. After today, she knew she could finally put it all to rest. With that realization came a quiet confidence she hadn't known before. She'd withstood so much in her life. This meeting in the Beyond, it would not break her. It was that plain, that simple. At peace with her inner strength and resolve, she rose up on an elbow and tapped him on his cheek.

"Another quick shower and we should go." She crawled off the bed despite his protests and narrowly escaped being drawn back into his arms.

附

Nathanael let the shower beat upon his skull as his heart pounded in his chest. *This is so not like me at all. I'm a pretty calm, cool, collected kinda guy, except for when I'm on a hunt. Why is my slow heart racing now?* Ariana. Her predicament worried him. What if she couldn't handle it in the Beyond? What if she could, but E.L. wiped all memories of him and the Brethren from her mind? What if he had to spend eternity knowing the woman he'd fallen in love with was out of reach?

Love? He'd fallen in love? Oh, yeah. He'd fallen hard. But he couldn't tell her. What good would it do either of them? It needed to remain a secret at least until after the meeting with E.L. If all things worked out, if she returned healthy and unharmed, even if her mortality was returned, he would ask to stay with her until the end of her days.

After putting on his jeans, he shoved a hand into his pants pocket and grabbed the delicate silver chain and charm he'd bought from Murati's Oddities shop. He hadn't meant to buy anything when he'd been there, but the charm had caught his eye and wouldn't let go. He knew immediately that it should be hers. Angel wings curved downward into the shape of a heart, encircling a sword with a diamond on its hilt. He hoped it would serve as a reminder of their connection to each other. Even if she didn't remember him once the meeting was over, at the very least, it would look beautiful around her neck.

"Hey, Red, come here." She'd been standing and staring out the window at the red rocks. Smiling, she did as he bade her.

"Yes, what is it?"

"I have something for you. I've had it for a little while, but I think now is the perfect time to give it to you."

"A present? You bought me a present?" She looked incredulous.

"Yes, I did. I saw it at the curiosity shop and couldn't resist." He snuck behind her and whispered in her ear. "Close your eyes and lift your hair."

"Wha— oh, okay." She laughed nervously and did as she was told, so the gentle curve of her neck lay bare for his hungry lips. He breathed her scent in, closed his eyes briefly, and laid feather-light kisses upon her. She purred, stretched up, and raked one hand through his damp locks.

He replaced his lips with the necklace, secured it, and traced the chain with his fingers so it rested just above the swell of her breasts. "Look in the mirror. Tell me what you think."

She turned to it and gasped. "Oh, Nate, it's beautiful! Angel wings, how perfect!" She leaned in closer. "And they make a heart around the sword. Is that a diamond in there? Oh my. You are amazing." She turned and dazzled him with her flushed cheeks. "I will wear this always. Thank you." She grabbed his hands and laced them with hers.

"Always? I like the sound of that." He leaned down to kiss her gently on the corners of her eyes, where tears had gathered. "I hate to say it, but we have to go. We can't stall this meeting any longer. Hold on tightly to me, Red, and I'll get you there safely. Close your eyes now, sweetness."

She wrapped her arms around his waist and squeezed. "Okay, I'm ready."

His wings fluttered open and wrapped protectively around her. He raised the two of them off the floor and began to spin like a top. As his speed increased exponentially, they became a human tornado and he heard her scream. The room fell away into a blur of color and then brilliant white light showered over them. He slowed their whirling to a stop, lowered them to the floor, and all was calm. Ariana tilted her head back and gawked at him, dazed and confused. Relief washed over him as he saw her come around a bit and that she didn't seem any worse for the harrowing trip.

"We're here."

"Ohhh...." She turned away from him, fell to her knees, and retched.

Chapter Eighteen

Am I dead? Am I dreaming? Are we in heaven? As Ariana regained her composure and capacity to hold the contents of her stomach down, she took a tentative glance around at the landscape. She rinsed her mouth with the spring water from a stream that crossed their path. Nathanael gave her a bandana to wipe it dry, and as she sat down on the gleaming ground, her gaze swept over the craggy, snow-topped mountains to her right. To her left stood a host of tall, marble buildings. All were awash with a white glow, making it seem as though she'd been transferred to a foggy English countryside with the sun ready to burst through. Before them loomed a huge temple-like structure with Roman pillars and innumerable steps leading to its entrance.

She leaned against her angel in amazement. "Nate, I don't think we're in Kansas anymore."

The rumble came first, and then his laughter. Peering up at him, she saw relief in his eyes. She giggled, too. "Rather cliché, I know, but the statement seemed to fit."

"Well, we are definitely not in Kansas anymore, sweetheart. I'm glad you're alive and standing on two feet. Speaking of which, are you able to walk on your own or do you need me to hold you up?"

She reached for him and he helped her to her feet. "Let me see if I have my sea legs yet." She tapped each foot on the shimmering sand. Solid. That was a good sign. "I'm okay. It's quite beautiful around here, Nate, although does this fog ever lift?"

"Fog? Oh, ha ha. Can't say that it does. But it's not really fog. It's more of a haze, wouldn't you say?"

"We can go with that. Sure." She snorted. "So where is everyone? Or wait—" she continued in a hushed whisper, "is everyone already here and they're just invisible to me?" She looked about and groped tentatively through the space around her.

Nathanael stood there shaking his head and laughing. *But really, what could he expect from me? A cowering little flower?* She was a fighter through and through. And she had questions about this place and wanted answers. He wiped his eyes and took her hands in his. "No, they are not invisible. No one is around because there is no one to be around, save for E.L. and his secretary. The only time you'll see others is when a meeting is called."

"So I suppose this is going to be a private meeting, then?"

"You suppose correctly." He kissed each palm and released one hand while putting a choke hold on the other. She didn't mind, though. The inevitable was upon them both. She knew it and needed all the support he could muster. "Time to head inside. It's up these stairs and through those huge stone-slab doors."

They walked in unison and silence, step by step, as the gravity of the situation had turned starkly real. Her doom or salvation loomed ever closer, and there were so many things she still needed to say. As if in slow motion, he extended a hand to open the door.

"Wait!" She heard herself cry out and tugged at him, refusing to go any farther.

Nathanael looked quizzically at her and must have mistaken her actions as those of fear, because he grabbed her to him in a fierce embrace. He murmured comforting words as he nuzzled her hair.

"Nate, I'm okay." She disentangled herself and went on. "You misunderstand. I need to say some things to you before we go inside. There are things I need you to know before...before whatever's gonna happen happens."

"Come on. You can tell me after."

"No, I can't. I mean, I might not be able to. I don't know what's gonna go down in there. So let me say my piece here and now."

He scrubbed his stubbly chin with his hand and nodded. "Okay, go ahead."

She started pacing in front of him. If she stood still, she would explode. "Okay, well, first of all, I want you to know how much I appreciate everything you've done for me. I'd be dead by now if it weren't for you, twice over at the very least. And you've helped me discover the truth of my past so I could put my parents' murders to rest." She stopped before him and grabbed his hands. "Secondly, I wanted to thank you for helping me trust again, for showing me that sex can be a beautiful thing and not something to loathe. Finally, I want to say how much I admire your strength. I know that you will manage your addiction with all the tenacity that a warrior and bounty hunter like you has inside."

She released his hands and rubbed her arms for comfort. "I care for you so much, Nathanael. Words can't even begin to describe what you mean to me. Love seems so inadequate. But it's the only word I've got. I'm in love with you, and wanted you to know." She turned away and leaned against a pillar.

In this, she regarded herself a coward, afraid to see the hint of rejection. If it were any other day, she never would have shared her true feelings about him. But she had a strange notion she'd regret it for the rest of her life to keep it inside. "I don't expect you to say anything back. I needed to say it, to get it out of me and out there in the ethos. I'm done, so let's g—"

The next thing she knew, she found herself spun around,

wrapped in Nathanael's arms, and smothered by a blistering-hot kiss. When he finally relinquished her lips, he pressed her up against the column and stood so close she could feel heat pouring off him in waves.

"Ariana Kupi, I've been in love with you ever since you equated my being in a bath towel to a Las Vegas strip show. You're sarcastic as hell, stubborn as a mule, and a royal pain in my ass most of the time. But Red, you are the only safe haven I've got in my maddening life, my own personal Elixxir, and you have kept me sane during the most trying of times." He cupped her face and regarded her with watery eyes. "I cannot, will not, lose you now. So, we hope for the best and fight for the rest. Okay?"

She could only nod, fearful that if she were to utter a sound, it would unleash a torrent of sobs, and she refused to give way. Grief mixed with joy and jubilation as she acknowledged the words he'd spoken. He was in love with her, too! Why, oh why, did this have to happen now? But he said he'd fight for them. She would, too. Taking a deep, shaky breath, she sniffled and caressed his cheek. "I'm ready."

He nodded and pushed open the monolithic doors. She followed him down an expansive white marble hallway filled with floor-to-ceiling angelic murals depicting scenes of serenity. They stopped at a desk that sat outside the big man's office.

"Hello, Shalisha, we are here to see E.L. He's expecting us."

"Nathanael, it's been a while. You're looking no worse for wear. Have a seat. He'll be right with you both."

"Thank you." He smiled pleasantly at the young woman, turned to Ariana, and grasped her hand in his. They moved over to a plush bench and sat down to wait for what seemed an inordinate amount of time. Her knees worked overtime in the bouncing department. Just as Nathanael placed his right hand across her knees to calm them, the doors to E.L.'s office opened.

By themselves.

She couldn't help but roll her eyes and snort at the egotistical display. That was enough to get her courage solidly in place. "Is he for real?" she whispered in his ear. "When I get back to Sedona and find a new place to live, I want that kind of door, too."

"Come on, wiseass. Time to meet the head honcho."

They got up from the bench and marched hand in hand into the office to sit before E.L. Nathanael reluctantly let go of her since the chairs were so far apart. As she leaned back in her seat, without his comfort to ease her racing heart, she sized up the enigmatic boss of the Brethren. A touch of salt and pepper in the hair, a bit of graying on the sides, a chiseled jaw line and straight nose. A white suit with a satiny sheen showed off a fit upper body. He made an imposing first impression. He seemed to be sizing her up, as well. She sat up a bit straighter and met his stare with confidence. *Good! Let him see I'm nothing to be trifled with.*

"Ariana Kupi."

"Yes, that's my name."

"You've had a most challenging life up to this point, shall we say?"

"I think that sums it up well enough."

"I regret we didn't know of you sooner, or we could have averted much trauma in your life."

"I appreciate that, but it's only served to make me stronger."

"Yes, and stronger is what saved two of my angels, and the Elixxir, from Evil's clutches. I thank you for both."

"You're welcome."

"We've got a bit of a conundrum, though. The Elixxir needed to be secured away, out of everyone's reach, but it's inside you at the moment, and making you ill."

"Is that going to be a problem? I mean, I don't want it inside me any longer, either. I know it was an impulsive move on my part, but it wasn't because I wanted to be immortal or anything like that. It just seemed like the right thing to do at the time."

"We need to retrieve it from your body somehow and restore your good health. That presents a problem. Extracting the Elixxir from your cellular structure is no easy task. But do it we shall."

Nathanael interjected with a shaky voice, "Could she die from this procedure?"

"I said it will be no easy task, not impossible. And she'll be fine after. So sit back in your seat and relax." He turned his attention back to her. "It takes only a few minutes for me to do it, during which time you will be in a sacred sleep. Otherwise, I fear the pain might overwhelm you. Once done, all will be as it was before."

"Oh, good." Relieved to hear so, she slumped back in her chair.

"Before what? All will be as it was before what, E.L.?"

"Now, Nathanael, I think you know better than to ask that question. What possible other outcome could you have envisioned other than a memory swipe?"

"Son of a—E.L., she deserves more than having all of this erased from her memory. She's done so much for us, and through this experience has learned how to handle her traumatic past. If you wipe her memory, she'll be back at square one! This is how you repay her for her multiple selfless acts?" He got up and stormed around the room, his fists opening and clenching in turn.

Ariana could tell a rush coursed through his veins, readying him for a fight. She stood up and glided over to him, obscuring his view of his boss.

"Nate, look at me," she said quietly, her voice controlled. "You need to stay calm. It will do neither of us any good to get worked up over this. Come sit down and I'll stand by your side. Let's see if we can reason with him."

He grumbled something unintelligible but listened to her and sat back down. She stood behind him and rested her hands on his shoulders.

"I can wipe her memories of the Brethren's existence without harming her progress in recovering from a traumatic childhood."

"I don't want her memory wiped, period, E.L. Take the

Elixxir. You don't have to take her memories."

"So it's like that, is it? You're in love with her?" His boss tapped his fingers on his desk. "I'm afraid that's not enough. She's mortal and cannot know of our existence. It's that simple."

"It's not just that I'm in love with her. She's the only one who can temper my addiction. In all my years of being on earth, no one has ever been able to do that. I need her more than you can know. And since you've been of no help to me, I have no choice but to seek out my own recovery and new life."

"I'll do what must be done, with or without your compliance. So which will it be, Nathanael?"

He shrugged out of Ariana's hold and lunged out of his seat toward E.L.

"Nate! No!"

With a wave of his hand, E.L. rendered him unconscious. His limp body dropped to the desktop and slid down to the floor.

"Oh, dear God! What have you done? You're as much a monster as Satan!" She scrambled to Nathanael's side and checked for a pulse, glaring at the imperious man as he sat calmly, shaking his head.

"He'll be fine. It's time."

As she felt a slow but steady beat that proved E.L.'s declaration, relief washed over her. She hugged her angel close to her and kissed him softly on his warm lips.

"Wait! My parents. Can you at least tell me if they are at peace now? Are they here?"

"They are indeed at peace. You need not worry. But they are not here. They reside in your heart and mind, forever and always. Now relax. We must begin."

Before she could even say goodbye to Nathanael, she drifted off to sleep by his side.

Chapter Nineteen

"Sikes and Sounds of Sedona, Ariana speaking, how can I help you? Sure, hold on, please." She slunk into Serena's office. "Hey, there's a call on line two for you. Someone asking about a bridal shower party here."

"Okay, thanks. How are you doing today, sweetie?"

She leaned against the door jamb, knowing she looked as pathetic as she felt. "Don't ask. Same as yesterday and the day before and the day before that, even. I'm not myself these days. I don't know, maybe it's the new apartment. Maybe I'm not settled yet."

"Could be. Sometimes a move can be a big adjustment, and it takes time to return to ourselves again."

"I think I'm missing something in my life, Serena. I know it sounds crazy, but there's this yearning inside of me, this longing for...for...oh, I don't know. There seems to be this hole in my life and nothing I do is filling it. It makes me so freakin' sad and pissed off at the same time. Something's gotta give. Hey, line two, lady. Enough about me and my miserable life." She laughed half-heartedly and returned to her desk.

Five o'clock couldn't come soon enough. Only fifteen minutes to go. She could leave early. Serena wouldn't mind. Ever since waking up in the hospital, apparently suffering from a case of dehydration, her best friend had been taking it easy on her. She gathered up her purse and walked out. She laughed as she recalled how many times her best friend had called her Callie instead of Ariana that day. They'd have a very nice lunch out on the many dollars she put in the Call Me By The Right Name jar. Thoughts of a piping hot pizza and an ice-cold beer drew her to her favorite pizza joint.

Driving back to her place with the mouth-watering smells of mushroom-and-pepperoni pizza wreaking havoc on her stomach, she ruminated over the sensational news out of Las Vegas. Her Uncle Eddie had been charged with embezzlement from the curiosity shop, but no one could find hide nor hair of him for the past few months. Hordes of reporters had descended upon her.

With her old identity back, she'd received all the things her parents had willed to her. A lovely condo overlooking the red rocks had been her huge purchase, aside from a new car. As she drove up her driveway, she shook her head. *Life sure is crazy sometimes.*

From the car she noticed something out of the ordinary. *Damn it!* She'd forgotten to leave the foyer light on. It wasn't dark out yet, but still, she liked to come home to lights on. It made her feel welcomed and at ease. She got out of the car and balanced the pizza in one hand while closing the car door with the other. Walking up the sidewalk, she dropped her keys. *I am so not meant to do more than one thing at a time!* She bent to pick them up.

"Let me help you with that."

That voice. I know that voice. Those hands. I know those hands! Afraid to prove her suspicions correct, she refused to look at the face to which they belonged. Instead, she cried out and stumbled backward, dropping the pizza as she slammed into a sign post.

"Is that any way to treat your long-lost bro, Callie?"

"Dennis. Wh...what the hell are you doing here?" Terror

ripped through her gut like a knife. Caught completely off-guard, she froze instead of doing what she'd been trained to do in self-defense classes.

He approached her and whipped a pistol out of his waistband, pointing it directly at her. "I saw you splashed all over the news and it got me thinking about all the pain and suffering I had to endure with you living in my house. I told you way back in the good old days that you owed me. Don't shout or make any awkward movements. Just walk over to your house with me. We'll go inside and come to a mutual understanding of how things are going to go down. Now."

He shoved the gun into her side and escorted her to the front door. "Open it."

Her hands shook so, she could barely put the key in the hole. But she did, and he shoved her inside, immediately locking the door behind them. "Sit down. On the steps."

She acquiesced and skittered silently to the stairs. It made no sense to argue at this point. "What do you want, Dennis?"

"What do I want?" He moved to loom over her. "Well, thanks for asking. You see, Evil's not quite done with you yet." He flashed two brilliant red orbs at her. "Seems you owe more than just me, now don't you?" He smiled like a twisted jack o'lantern, but then he turned quite serious. "I want money. Lots of it. And you're gonna get it for me."

What's the matter with his eyes? And evil's not done with me? What does that mean? The man is off his rocker. "The banks are closed. I can't get you the tons of money you want until tomorrow."

"That's all right, baby sis, we got all night then to reminisce and get...reacquainted."

"You've got another think coming if you believe for one second I'm gonna let you anywhere near me like...like that." She scooted up a couple of steps.

"Oh, I'll be coming all right." He laughed a maniacal laugh, and she could have sworn he'd grown a couple inches taller. A flash of a memory teased at her mind and just as quickly it vanished. "You can start things off right by giving me that necklace."

"What?" She touched absently at the charm. She'd found it around her neck upon awakening in the hospital. She still had no clue who'd given it to her, but it meant something to her nonetheless. "No. I won't."

"Yes, Callie. You will because I said so, and so does this here gun." He aimed it at her head.

"Okay. Okay." She unfastened the clasp and handed the chain and charm over to him. He shoved them in his jacket pocket.

"That's a good little girl. Now," he said in a husky voice, "take off your clothes."

"No."

"Yes." He brought his gun up again to point at her chest and stared her down.

"You'll have to kill me, Dennis. I won't do it."

She glared right back and found the courage to go for broke, because she'd be damned if he would ever touch her body again while she was alive to feel it. She took a deep breath and kicked at his hand with the gun. It fired off a shot before flying out of his hand.

"You bitch! You're gonna pay double for this!"

He lunged at her and she rolled to the side, scrambling back down the steps to the front door. He grabbed her foot and her body slammed into the floor. She kicked fiercely at his hands to try to release her leg, but couldn't, and looked around for something to throw at him. The gun lay almost within reach, so she wriggled across the floor and managed to grab it. Turning back toward him, she got off one stray shot before he let go of her leg and pounced. He grabbed for the gun and they struggled for possession. She wouldn't dare let it go. He wrapped his hand around hers and forced it to turn inward.

"No!" she shrieked, realizing his intention.

He pressed his fingers against hers and another round went off.

"Uh!" Surprise flooded over her, and then searing pain tore through her chest, making it so she could barely breathe. He'd made her shoot herself! She released the gun and her hands flopped to the tile beneath her.

"I win this time. Score one for Evil! Ha! So, I'm thinking I need to go to Plan B. That's all right. Know what I'm gonna do? I'm gonna help you write your last will and testament. And you're gonna sign it, bequeathing me all your worldly possessions."

Through the blur of pain she watched him scribble something on a scrap of paper and walk over to her blood-soaked body.

"Take this pen and sign your name right here." He pointed to a blank spot on the note and put the pen in her hand. She dropped it. "Come on! You better sign this before you die."

"Can't...." Her breath had turned shallow and raspy, her skin ice cold.

"I'll help you, then." His hand wrapped around hers and moved it.

"There, all done. Thanks a bunch, sis. Your debt has been paid. You can die happy now."

"Save me...." Her lips moved. She expelled air, but no sound came out. Her world went dark.

cg

Nathanael burst through the door to the condo and Raphael rushed in after. There was no time to knock. The plea came in as the woman's soul left her body. Raphael found her lying unconscious in a pool of blood. He immediately began his healing efforts. Nathanael left him to his work and stalked around the place, tracking any clue.

Something glinted from the carpet on the stairs. He charged over to find a necklace, a chain with an angel wing and sword charm on it. He picked it up and his senses went into high gear as a flood of memories descended upon him. The perpetrator of the crime had been possessed by Evil. He knew this woman and had wanted to rape her as some kind of retribution. He planned to head to Vegas after stealing money from her bank account.

This woman. Other memories, personal recollections, cascaded down his neural pathways like a watershed, knocking him on his ass. This wasn't just some woman. This was *his* woman! Ariana! He ran over to find her lifeless despite all of Raphael's efforts. His hands trembled as he caressed her cheek.

"Raphael. Save her, brother. Bring her back. She's my woman. My Elixxir. I can't lose her."

"What do you mean?"

Through their threaded connection as Brethren, he shared memories that had been erased from their collective remembrances.

"I'm doing my best. Find whoever did this and I'll do all I can. Go."

Nathanael raced out the front door and took to the skies. He knew exactly where to find the bastard. And he knew who he was, too. Dennis. He would surely die tonight at the hands of Brethren justice.

Alighting at the entrance to a dark, dead-end alley in a seedy section of Phoenix, he tucked away his wings, knowing at the other end Dennis and an underage hooker were getting it on. He stalked toward the two of them, the addictive rush pumping hard through his system, feeding the rage that had built since he'd left Ariana in Raphael's capable hands. In mere moments he arrived at the couple. Dennis had his pants down around his ankles and she knelt on the ground before him.

"Dennis! I've come for you. Say hello to your own personal angel of death." In a grand display, he unfurled his massive, luminous wings and unsheathed his sword. Dennis shoved the prostitute away from him and staggered back against a Dumpster.

"Who the fuck are you?"

He watched as the witless man fumbled with pulling up his pants and closing his zipper. "I'm Nathanael, Brethren Warrior, the first and the last angel you're ever gonna see, fuckhead. So get a good, long look, you sorry excuse for brain matter."

"What the fuck are you going on about? I have no beef with you. I don't even know you."

"But I know you, you sick, perverted sex offender."

"She told me she was eighteen! I swear it!" His eyes were wide and he held his hands up in submission.

Nathanael turned to her. "Why are you still here? Run, and don't look back. Run home and get out of this whoring business." The girl picked up her purse, took off her shoes, and ran all the way up the alley. He turned his attention back on Dennis. Raising his sword, he began doling out his revenge.

He flicked the sword twice within seconds, and Dennis let out a howl as his hands flew up to the sides of his head, where his ears used to be.

"That's for not listening to Ariana when she said no."

Next, he jabbed and skewered his manhood. The man let out a wail so loud it actually irritated Nathanael's sensitive hearing.

"That's for sticking your dick in places it never should have gone."

With his addiction being fed right now, invincibility controlled him. "Dennis, for the crimes you have perpetrated against children, I hereby sentence you to Brethren justice, swift and permanent."

"No! Don't kill me. It's not my fault. I'm possessed by Satan. I'm sick. I need help. I'll do anything you say. "Dennis tried to climb up the Dumpster, but his pants had fallen down again and he kept sliding on the smooth metal. He turned around and his face filled with horror.

Nathanael raised his sword high in the air and brought it down in an arch, slicing straight through Dennis' neck. His lifeless body crumpled to the ground as his head dropped like a bowling ball and rolled away. The blade shimmered a fiery orange as it absorbed Dennis's blood, and Nathanael fell to his knees in agony, trembling and fighting against the need for more bloodshed.

"Ariana!" he cried out in desperation, knowing it to be a fruitless endeavor. "Ariana! Help me." A voice touched his soul and a ray of hope dared to break through his inner storm.

"I'm here with you, Nate. Don't give in to the rush. Sense me inside you instead and let that be enough. Come to me."

"Ariana?" He calmed a bit more and raised himself to his feet. Before him she stood, a ghost, a spirit, a soul. And he wept. She'd left him. But he wouldn't give her up without a fight. He beckoned to her. "Come back to me, Red! Don't leave me here alone, without you. I love you. I need you."

"And I need you more." She offered a hand to touch him, and he to her, but they passed right through each other.

"Raphael is working so hard to bring you back to me."

The ephemeral visage nodded, smiled, and faded into nothingness.

"No!" he roared, and shot up into the sky, breaking all kinds of speed records to make it back to her place. He refused to believe she'd gone for good.

ↀ

"I've got a pulse! It's slow and steady." Raphael lifted his fingers from Ariana's neck and turned to Serena to kiss her soundly. "Wife of mine, I love you with every fiber of my being, but tonight, I adore you as a servant cherishes his goddess. Thank you."

"Aren't you the sweetest?" She gave him a peck. "I couldn't very well lose my best friend. That would be absolutely unacceptable. She deserves far better than the messed-up life she's been dealt and to leave it in such a horrifying way. She's acted selflessly for the Brethren and, in my opinion, belongs with us. If E.L. has words about it, let him take it up with me."

"Add that to the list of why I love you. You've grown a huge pair!" They laughed together.

Nathanael watched from the corner, silently brooding. His thoughts, consumed by Ariana's probable demise, deafened him from hearing the couple's exchange until their laughter shook him free. He stormed straight over to Ariana, who still lay unconscious. "How can you laugh at such a time as this? She's...she's...."

"Alive! She's going to be fine." Raphael placed a comforting hand on his arm to calm him, and continued in a hushed voice. "I had to call Serena in. Brother, she died. Before you and I even arrived. Thank goodness for Serena and her gift of regeneration."

"Serena, how can I ever repay you for bringing her back?" Tears stung, and she knelt down to give him a squeeze.

"No thanks necessary. She belongs with us. You know it and I know it. I'm sure if E.L. hadn't wanted this to happen, he would have done something about it already."

"I'll never forgive him for what he's done to us." Nathanael bristled as he stroked his woman's hair and looked longingly at her still form.

"Now I can understand this is not the way you wanted things to go, but look what you've both gained. She's immortal now! You can spend the rest of eternity being angry, or understand E.L. takes some pretty strange paths to an end that has been more than acceptable to all of us."

"He could have given her immortality before, without all the drama. How she must have suffered simply to end up at the same eventuality. It's ridiculous."

"But he saved the honor of granting her immortality for me. I am truly grateful to have been the one to bestow it upon her. She's my best friend, my sister. And now we get to spend eternity together. What a perfect ending. At least I think so. Hopefully, she'll believe the same when she wakes up."

They all stared at Ariana's face, waiting for her to stir. "When do you think she will? Wake up, I mean?"

"She should be rousing anytime now." Raphael checked her vitals again. "Good and strong. Her heart beat slow, perfect."

"Will she remember me, Raph?"

"I honestly don't know. Hey, she's coming around."

"Mmm...mmm. Oh, geez. What am I doing on the floor? Raphael, what are you doing here? Serena?" She shot up to a sitting position. "Holy crap, what's this all over my shirt? Blood? Okay, somebody talk to me!"

"Calm down, sweetie. Everything is fine now." Serena put a soothing hand on her head.

"Fine *now*? What about *before* now?" She closed her lids, trying to remember what had happened to her. Bits and pieces floated in and out. She heard gunshots in her mind and looked at Raphael. "I was shot. Okay, that explains the blood. But by whom?" She scrunched her eyes shut again and Dennis's face burst through the haze and she grabbed Raphael's hand. "That son of a bitch. Dennis forced my hand so I would shoot myself. Where is he? Has he run off? Do the police know? And why do I feel perfectly fine now?" She lifted her shirt with trembling hands and saw no sign of any wounds. Rather than putting the bloody mess back on, she opted to remove the whole shirt. Bra, bikini top, same thing, relatively, she thought. *But what the hell is going on around here?*

Her best friend had a strange look on her face. So did Raphael. And the other guy, she thought his name was Nathan, or something like that, looked like he'd lost his favorite puppy dog. She crossed her arms over her chest and sighed.

"You have exactly five seconds to tell me everything. Five, four...."

"Okay. Dennis has been dealt with. You don't have to worry about him anymore. When Raphael got here, you were, well, dead. He called me immediately, I rushed over, and we brought you back."

"Whoa. You...you brought me back? With a defibrillator thing like we have at the store? Boy, I literally owe you my life. The two of you. Thank you so much. But the wounds—" She kept touching her stomach and chest trying to find any signs of bullet holes.

"There's more, sweetie."

"There's always more, isn't there?" She shook her head and sighed.

"The way I brought you back is, well, unusual. Nathanael, Raphael, and I are immortal and I have special abilities that enabled me to bring you back from the dead. And now, you're immortal, too."

Ariana stared at her best friend and blinked a few times. Then she laughed hysterically. "Oh, you're good! That's your best joke yet. I'm being punked, aren't I? And your name is Nathanael? Right? I knew it was something with a Nathan in it. You're in on this, too? Oh, you folks slay me. You really do. Okay, time to spill it. How could I have been shot dead without so much as a scratch on me now?"

Serena opened her mouth to say something, but Nathanael cut in. "I found this on the steps. I believe it belongs to you." Her charm necklace dangled from his hand.

"Oh, thank you! I don't know what I would have done if it'd been lost. It's very special to me." She moved to grab it from him, but he held on to it. She frowned. "It helps if you let it go."

He gathered both her hand and necklace in his own hands and wouldn't let go. "Do you remember me, Ariana? Do you remember us?"

"Wha—oh." The room spun and colors swirled like paint in a mixing jar. Had she not been held up by him, she would have toppled over.

Memories of all kinds crashed down upon her like a tidal wave. But the ones that stuck, the ones that refused to float off again, were the memories of how connected she had been to Nathanael, and of being in love with this man, this...angel...before her. The funhouse ride slowed to a stop and all she could see was the one she'd longed for the past few weeks.

"Oh, my God, Nathanael." Tears trailed down her cheeks, but she refused to wipe them away. "I remember everything now. Everything! It's been you I've missed so much, but I...I didn't know you." She beat her chest with her fist. "My heart, it ached, and I couldn't figure out why." She shook her head in disbelief, and touched his cheek with trembling fingers.

"Thank God, I've finally got you back, Red," he said gruffly. Releasing his wings, he pulled her onto his lap and enclosed them both inside. She didn't know who initiated the kiss first, but all coherent thought left her, and the only thing that remained was a primal need to possess and consume this creature she'd fallen deeply in love with.

"We'll leave you two to get reacquainted, right Raphael?"

"Yeah, we have some business to take care of. We'll catch up with you both later."

Ariana waved them off and heard bits of a debate over what they should do about the busted door. They decided it could still close, sort of, and would do for now.

"So you're in the big leagues now. Gone immortal on me." He looked down upon her with those stunning, blinking emeralds in utter adoration.

"Yup, I guess I can nag you for the rest of eternity, like any good wife."

"Oh, is that so?" He raised an eyebrow and tickled her in the ribs.

"Yes, sir. I'll be able to harp on you endlessly about how you have too many clothes on in the house. Sort of like you do right now. Could you do something about that, sweetheart?" She batted her lashes and bit the tip of her index finger.

"Why, Red, I do believe I like your kind of nagging." He stood her up and quickly stripped his pants off. "And now, how about a little game of Bounty Hunter? I'm the hunter and you're my bounty. Better run." He wiggled his eyebrows. She squealed and dashed up the stairs, throwing her bra in the air. When she reached the landing, she took off the rest of her clothes and ran into her master bathroom straight to the shower.

"Ha ha! I know where you are, little Red. I got your brain my hand and can sense where you're hiding."

"Hey! No fair!" She quickly covered her mouth. "Aw, shit. That didn't help any either, now did it?" Her breath quickened with each moment that went by, and she giggled with anticipation.

"Come out, little Red. I've got a treat for you."

His message caressed her ear, and she thought his low-timbred voice damned sexy. Heat spread throughout her body and a light buzz made her feel as though she'd drunk the perfect margarita. She stepped out from the shower curtain and found him in the doorway, arms raised to the top of the door frame, like Atlas holding the world on his shoulders, and looking very much like the Greek god himself. His beauty stole her breath away. She took a step toward him, a moth to a flame.

"You're more than treat enough. In fact, I'm gonna keep you closer to me than my chocolate from here on out."

He lowered his arms to his sides. His gaze spoke of raw need and she could see him tremble with sexual restraint. "Come to me. I'm feeling kinda strange. Out of sorts."

She closed the distance between them, and slithered up his body, kissing and licking until she stood on her tiptoes to kiss him full on the mouth.

He slid his hands around her waist and drew her even closer to him. "That's a whole lot better. I must've been in need of my Elixxir."

She smiled and pushed him backward down the hall to her bedroom and onto her bed. Falling on top of him, she righted herself and pushed up on his chest so her hair curtained their faces. "Looks like the hunter's become *my* bounty, angel boy. Gonna have to lock you up and throw away the key."

"Promise?" He ran his fingers lightly in circles on her back.

"Uh huh."

"I got a promise for you."

"Oh yeah?" She kissed him lightly on the corners of his mouth. "What's that?"

"I promise that from now on the only addiction I will ever fall prey to is you."

"You're in luck." She smiled. "We've the rest of eternity for you to fulfill that promise."

~ABOUT THE AUTHOR~

It was the mystique of Arizona's history and landscape that called to Deena and catapulted her career as an author. When she's not writing novels and poetry in the wee, small hours of the morning or in the deep, dark of night, Deena teaches language arts to middle school students. She currently lives in Gilbert with her husband and two children, but New Jersey will always tug at the heartstrings.

Visit Deena online at:
www.deenaremiel.com
www.facebook.com/DeenaRemielAuthor
www.twitter.com/deenaremiel

Trinity
Book One of the Brethren Series

One way or another, terror will reign tonight.

School teacher and single mom, Emma Livingston, has been through hell—and back so she thinks. While dealing with the night terrors and active imagination of her five-year old daughter, Hannah, she attempts to lead a normal life. That is, until the demon from those nightmares pays her a visit, too, and threatens both of their lives. Desperate, she reaches out for help—and finds Michael waiting.

Michael D'Angelo is known to everyone in Prophet's Point, Arizona, as their loving elementary school principal. But to The Brethren, he is the most powerful Protector. Immortal and angelic does not mean he's without doubts or fears, as protecting Emma and Hannah from Evil tests his ability to fight his tortured past.

As the Trinity is formed, ancient secrets are revealed and faith is tested. When a prophecy is exposed, Hannah becomes the main target and Emma wonders if a normal life will ever be possible again. Hope is like an anchor, but can a mother, her daughter, and an angel overcome the evil determined to annihilate the world?

Relic
Book Two of the Brethren Series

Raphael, a Brethren Savior, an angel with a forgotten past, has lost his power to heal and is on a self-imposed guilt trip to get it back. If he can't, his tour of eternal duty as Brethren Savior will be revoked. On his journey, he winds up enmeshed in a web of attempted murder and resurrection, all thanks to a woman he's only seen in a photograph and by chance on an Arizona desert hiking trail.

Serena Sikes is a wanted woman. Desired by "undesirables" for a gift her brother gave her—a stolen relic with suspected healing powers. Hunted down in the Arizona desert and left for dead, she is found by none other than the angel who cannot heal.

Three souls bound together by an ancient relic, bound by a timeless gift, and bound by a love that is eternal.

Available in ebook and print from Decadent Publishing
www.decadentpublishing.com

www.ingramcontent.com/pod-product-compliance
Lightning Source LLC
Chambersburg PA
CBHW060055150626
46556CB00017BA/745